Rain's Theory 2

K.C. Mills

Text **LEOSULLIVAN** to 22828 to join our mailing list!

To submit a manuscript for our review, email us at leosullivanpresents@gmail.com

-1-

Rain

"Theory, wake up. Please wake up." I called his name, but was afraid to touch him. I could see the blood pouring from his body and didn't want to make it worse, so I didn't dare touch him. Blood was everywhere. My heart was pounding and Theory wasn't responding.

I grabbed his phone and tried to steady my hands enough to go to his recent call log, and Frank's number was the first one I found, so I touched it and then the button to connect the call. It took a minute, but Frank's voice finally came through.

"What up Theory?"

"Is this Frank?" My voice was shaky, but I managed to get the words out.

"Who is this?" I could tell that Frank was in defensive mood.

"It's Rain, I need you to come to my apartment complex. Theory just got shot and he told me to call you."

"Shot, the fuck you mean shot, what's the address?"

"2400 Sinclair Parkway. We're in the parking lot. I didn't see anything because he covered my body with his, but I heard the car leaving. They shot him more than once, and he won't wake up. Should I call the ambulance?"

"No, I'm on my way. I can be there in like ten minutes. Try to wake him up, keep talking to him. Are you okay, did you get hit?"

"No I'm fine, just hurry up. Please."

After I ended the call with Frank, my attention was right back on Theory again.

"Thee, please wake up, Frank's on his way, so I need you to wake up." I reached for his face and as my finger glided across his skin, it was like my mind went blank. I couldn't process what was happening, no matter how hard I tried. When I heard Frank calling my name, I blinked hard and snapped back to reality, which meant that I had been out of focus for a while because Frank told me that it would take him at least ten minutes to get here.

Frank was snatching open Theory's door and pulling him out, while Niles opened mine and grabbed my arm.

"What are you doing?" I asked, looking at Niles and then Frank, who was struggling to lift Theory and position him into the car that they had arrived in.

"Just get out," Niles said forcefully, yanking on my arm again with a little too much aggression, so I snatched away from him, giving him a look that dared him to touch me again. By this time, Frank had Theory in the passenger side of his car and was shutting the door.

He eyed Niles before he focused on me. "Rain, I need you to do me a favor. It's real important. Get in the car. We have to get him out of here and right now." Frank's eyes were sympathetic, but I could also see that he was stressed about the situation. I didn't know what was going on, but if Theory trusted him, then I trusted him. I nodded, walked over to the car that Frank had just put Theory in, and climbed into the back seat.

Niles got in the other side while Frank went through Theory's truck. I watched as he got my purse and camera bag, Theory's phone, and then found two guns from somewhere. He opened his trunk, put the guns inside, before he got in on the driver's side. He handed me Theory's phone, my purse and camera bag, and then pulled out of the parking lot. A few minutes later, Frank was on the phone making calls. The first one, all he said was we're on our way and then hung up. The next, he gave someone instructions on where to pick up Theory's truck and then hung up. I could see him watching me in his rearview mirror. My eyes mostly stayed focused on Theory, who still hadn't woken up.

"Did you see them; did you see their faces?" I could hear Niles's voice, but I was so focused on Theory that I didn't respond to him until he yelled my name.

"Rain, did you see the two guys that shot at you?" Niles had his hand on my arm and I looked down at it, causing him to let me go.

"No, Theory pulled me down and then covered my body with his, so I didn't see anything," I answered him, but my eyes were still on Theory.

"Are you sure you didn't see them?" What the fuck! Why was he so worried about that?

"No, damn it, I told you I didn't," I yelled, but this time I turned to face him.

Frank glanced at us in the rearview mirror, but he was more focused on Niles versus me. He looked at Niles strangely and if I had to guess, the look in his eyes was suspicion.

"Are we going to the hospital?" I thought it was strange to me that Frank didn't want me to call an ambulance.

"No, we have our own doctor. If we go to the hospital, they'll have to call the cops to report it and we don't need that," Frank said.

Again, Frank's eyes were on me from his rearview mirror, but I didn't say anything; I just focused on Theory again. I felt like I couldn't breathe. If he couldn't breathe, then I couldn't breathe, so right now my chest was tight and I felt like I was struggling with each breath.

About twenty minutes later, we were at the back of an office complex. Frank pulled right up to the curb and there waiting, was who I assumed, was the doctor that Frank mentioned. He was a nerdy looking white guy, dressed in khakis and a pale blue polo shirt. He was standing next to a gurney and the second Frank stopped the car, he rushed over to the side that Theory was on, and opened the door to examine him.

"How many shots?' he asked, looking at Frank.

"I don't know, I just got him here. Move, damn it!" Frank yelled, as he pushed the guy out the way and ducked into the car, trying to get Theory out. I got out and watched as he moved him.

"The fuck you standing there for, help me get him out," Frank yelled at Niles.

Nikes looked at him like he wasn't feeling the way Frank was handling him, but did as Frank asked. I could tell that he wasn't happy. Something was up with him. The doctor placed his hands on the gurney and moved it next to the car, so that Frank and Niles could get Theory on it. Once they had him situated, the doctor rushed him inside, while I stood there frozen. What the hell was going on?

"Rain," Frank touched my arm, and then waited for me to respond. His approach was much subtler than Niles, and I appreciated that. I didn't know why, but that one gesture finally got to me, and I broke down. The tears started falling and I was struggling to catch my breath.

Frank hesitated for a minute, like he was torn about what to do next, but then pulled me into his chest, and wrapped his arms around me. He stood there with me until I snatched away. What was I doing? Theory was fine and he would be so disappointed if he thought that for one second, I didn't believe that. I wiped my face with the back of my hand and took a deep breath.

"I'm sorry," I mumbled and then took a step back. Frank looked at me confused, before he spoke.

"I need you to do me a favor. Don't talk to Niles about what happened. If he asks you anything, just say that you don't remember," Frank said.

"Why?" Now I was confused. Niles and Theory were friends, business partners, but Frank was acting like he didn't trust him. Hell, I didn't really trust him either, but I didn't know him. They did.

"I just got a bad feeling. I hope like hell I'm wrong but for now, just trust me on this," Frank said.

"Fine, I need to go see him," I said and started walking to the building. I didn't know what they had going on and I really didn't care. The only thing that mattered to me right now was that Theory was okay. Once I knew he was good, then I could think about something else, but for now, all my energy belonged to making sure Theory made it out of this.

When we made it inside, Niles was in the corner on the phone. He looked at us, turned his back and lowered his voice. I could see Frank out of the corner of my eye, and his body was tense, along with the fact that his expression turned hard.

"Where is he?" I asked, looking right at Frank.

He grabbed my hand, leading me through a set of office doors, down a hallway where there were several exam rooms. He moved past several of them, checking each one until he found the one that Theory was in. His clothes were cut off him and hanging from the gurney he was lying on, while the doctor was leaning over his body, inspecting it. Theory was now hooked up to an IV and several other machines, but his body looked like it had no signs of life. If it weren't for the rhythm of the monitor that the he was hooked to, I would have broken down again. And besides, I refused to be weak. I couldn't, not now, because whatever strength I had, Theory needed and I wasn't going to fail him. After years of him being there for me, watching over me, protecting me, it was finally my turn, and I was not about to let him down.

"He was hit three times, once in the back, once in the side and once in the shoulder. It's pretty bad; whoever did this really wanted him dead." The doctor glanced at me first, and then Frank, as he spoke.

"But, he's good though, right?" Frank asked.

"I can't tell you that right now, but I'll do what I can. It's going to take some time, so you might want to get comfortable.

Frank nodded and started towards the door. When I didn't move, the doctor looked at me and spoke. "It's best if you wait out there," he said, as he pressed on Theory's side, causing a gush of blood to expel from it.

"Rain, come on ma, we can wait out there." I didn't move though, not until I felt Frank's hand on my shoulder. I looked up at him and he was just as worried as I was. Completely different reaction from Niles. Niles seemed more concerned about the shooters than he did about Theory.

I walked over to Theory and kissed the side of his face, before I whispered in his ear, "You can't leave me. Nothing about me works without you." Then I kissed his lips before I turned to the doctor.

"You better figure this out. He doesn't die. Do you hear me?" He glanced at Frank before he laid eyes on me again. He simply nodded and I walked away. Once Frank and I were back in the waiting room, Niles looked at both of us.

"How is he?"

I didn't bother responding, I just sat down and let my elbows rest on my legs before I lowered my head in my hands.

I heard Frank answer as he sat down next to me. "Don't know yet."

He leaned back because I could feel his arm on the back of my chair.

Rain's Theory 2   K.C. Mills

"So, what's next?" Niles asked.

"We fucking wait." I could hear the agitation in Frank's voice.

"I can't just sit here, I'm about to go hit the streets. We need to figure out who did this shit. You good here?" Niles asked. All I could think about was the fact that Theory was in there fighting for his life, and this asshole was about to die to get out of here.

"I don't give a fuck what you do right now," Frank said.

"Damn nigga, what that fuck is your problem?" Niles asked, causing me to lift my head and look at both of them.

"Just go see what you can find out. I'll hit you when we know what's going on here." I could tell that Frank was trying to calm himself.

"Yeah aight, do that," Niles said, before he glanced at me and then Frank. "I called Anderson to come get me, so you can keep the car."

Frank didn't respond, he just let his head fall back, closed his eyes, and after a few minutes of awkwardly standing there, Niles finally walked out the door. It was clear that a line had been drawn and sides chosen. I just didn't really know what that meant for Theory.

*****

I could hear voices, but my eyes were so heavy that they literally felt as if they were glued shut, because I was trying to open them, but I had to struggle to do it.

When I finally had a visual, I could see Frank standing a few feet away from where I was sitting. He had one arm folded across his chest while the other was vertical, with his fist balled up covering his mouth. His eyes were burning a hole through the doctor as he listened to him talking. Frank's body language made me nervous, so I didn't move. I just watched their exchange, while it felt like I was holding my breath.

A few minutes passed and then I watched as Frank nodded, shook the doctor's hand, and then the doctor disappeared into the hallway that lead to the exam room where Theory was. Frank stood there and I could tell that he was deep in thought, and that sacred me. I couldn't handle any bad news, so I sat there watching, afraid to ask for an update, and when Frank laid eyes on me, his hard expression softened as much as it could.

"How is he?" I asked.

"He's stable." Frank walked over and sat down next to me. He covered my hand with his, which to me, was a sign that I needed to worry.

"Stable, what does that mean? Stable could go either way, right?" I asked, looking Frank right in the eyes. I needed to see the sincerity behind his eyes when he answered.

"He had some pretty serious injuries, so for now we wait. I'm waiting for the van so that we can move him to his house. I have people set up to come take care of him, but he's gonna be okay Rain. I believe that and I need you to believe that." Frank made sure he I believed what he was saying when he looked into my eyes. Not long after, the van arrived with a medical team to get Theory, and we were pulling up at an unfamiliar property, which had me confused.

"I thought we were going to Theory's house; who's place is this?" I asked, when we pulled into the driveway of a very nice brick house. It was small and in no way did it compare to Theory's house.

"This is his house; one of them, anyway. You know how he is about his privacy." Frank opened the door to get out, so I did too. He had someone pick up the car that he drove Theory to the doctor in, and they delivered a black-on-black Ranger Rover which I assumed belonged to Frank, because it had his things in it.

Once I was out the truck, I followed behind Frank as he walked to the front door. He keyed something on the security pad and then the door opened. The men who were in the van with Theory were behind us, and carried him on a gurney into the house, down a hall, and into a bedroom. I stood in the living room looking around. The place was nice, decorated similar to the house that I knew belonged to Theory, so I could tell that he owned this one too. But, I was confused about why he had two homes.

Frank had gone with the men carrying Theory, and I assumed it was to go get him set up. A few minutes later, Frank was in front of me.

"I'll stay with you until the team gets here, and then I'm going to meet Diamond to get your things. I assume you're staying here?"

He looked in my eyes and waited for me to respond. I nodded and he continued.

"I have some things to take care of and then I'll be back with your things. You're good here. Nobody knows about this house, so if anybody is after Thee, they won't know to look here. I don't know what's going on yet, so it's best if I keep him out of sight for a minute. You good with that?"

"Do you think that? Do you think that whoever did this is still after him?" I asked.

"I don't know ma, that's what I need to go find out, so for now, I need whoever did this to think that they actually accomplished what they set out to do."

"What about Niles?" I had to ask. I didn't trust him and I was seriously thinking that he had something to do with this. The second I said his name, Frank's jaw tightened.

"He doesn't know about this house and I haven't told him anything yet. As far as he's concerned, Theory didn't make it."

I could tell from the expression on Frank's face that he was feeling the same way about Niles, that I was.

"Can I go in there with him?" I asked.

"Yeah, come on."

I followed Frank down the hall and we both stopped in the doorway of what appeared to be the master bedroom, based on the setup. My eyes roamed the room briefly, but stopped once they reached Theory, who was in the center of a king sized bed that sat high off the ground. He had monitors hooked up to him that had to have already been in the room, because the guys that transported him, only carried Theory.

There was a nurse that I hadn't noticed before, checking his pulse. She must have been in the van with them, or already here waiting. I moved closer to the bed and surveyed his body. He looked peaceful, but my chest felt tight the longer I looked at him.

"I'm about to head out, are you sure you're going to be oaky?" Frank's voice pulled my focus away from Theory.

"I'll be fine."

Frank looked around the room and then at Theory, before he inhaled, releasing it slowly. "There's food in the kitchen and if you need anything, call me. You've got his phone, right?"

"Yeah, I'll be fine. Go do whatever you have to do," I said. At this point, I just wanted all these people out of here. I needed to be with Theory, alone, without everyone watching us and checking on him.

"Okay, I'll be back; it will probably be late, but I'll be back."

"Frank, I'll be fine."

He finally left and the room cleared out. I asked the nurse if it was okay for me to lay with him, but honestly I didn't really care what she told me because I was doing it anyway. If he could feel my body next to his, the rhythm of my heart beating, then I believed that he would be okay. Ever since we were kids, Theory always told me that my heartbeat set the pace of his. He said that was how he always knew what I was thinking or feeling. If I was afraid, then his heartbeat raced out of control just like mine, and when I was sad, hurt, or lonely, his slowed to a snail's pace, barely noticeable. So, surely if he felt my heart beating next to his, then he would have to be okay, right?

I kicked off my shoes, pulled the covers back, and moved slowly towards his body. His bare chest was bandaged on the side, as well as his shoulder, reminding me of how bad things really were. As carefully as I could, I inched closer to him and he didn't move. His body was warm, which calmed me a little, so I grabbed his hand and laced my fingers through his, letting my head rest on the pillow next to his, and closed my eyes. I was exhausted, just wanted to rest and before long, my body shut down and I was drifting.

Theory

"Theory, let's just go." Rain was almost in tears but I didn't care. My pulse was racing and I was seeing red. I could see the fear in her eyes, but even if mine were closed, I could feel it radiating from her body and creeping into mine. That was how we worked, I didn't understand it, but I accepted it, and right now I was about to handle the reason why she was feeling this way.

"I gripped the metal pipe I was holding so tightly that my knuckles should have been white and when Rain touched my arm, her pulse entered my body.

"Stay here," I commanded, looking right into her eyes and pointing my finger towards the alley we were standing in.

"Thee, please don't. I'm fine now, let's just go."

"You heard me Rain, I said stay here." I lifted the metal pipe and turned to walk away. I could hear her sobbing behind me, but I couldn't worry about that. I needed these niggas to know that she was off limits, whether I was with her or not, and the only way that was going to happen was if I stepped to them.

When I rounded the corner, I could see the two guys that tried to pull Rain into the abandoned building that entered into the alley, where she was waiting for me. If I hadn't shown up, then I knew exactly what would have happened. It further confirmed that I had to find a way to get us off the streets.

"Yo," I yelled, as I moved towards them. The fact that there were two of them meant that I had to act fast and catch them off guard, so the second I was close enough, I swung the pipe at the first one. I reached with so much force that it knocked him out. His body hit the ground, while his friend squared up, ready for me. I was fortunate enough that he was holding, because he swung at me instead of reaching for his heat. When I stepped back he missed, but I didn't when I landed a blow to the side of his head with the pipe I was holding. He grabbed the spot I hit, but I kept swinging until he hit the ground and screamed for mercy.

When my arms got tired, I leaned down and pressed the pipe I was holding into his chest. "She's off limits. If I see you even look her way, I promise you that you will regret it." I looked him right in his eye and could see the hate brewing. This wasn't over and I knew it, but for now, I had delivered a message. I lifted the pipe and lowered it to my side as I turned to leave. When I laid eyes on Rain again, she ran to me and held onto me like she was consumed with a fear that she was never going to see me again. After I let go, I grabbed her hand and we walked away. That was the last time we talked about it. She never asked what happened and I never told her. All she knew was that I had her and that was all that mattered.

When I opened my eyes, my body felt heavy. There was pain covering every inch of it, but I didn't care. If I could feel pain, then I was alive. I was disoriented and it took me a minute to realize where I was because the room was dark, aside from a light glowing that surrounded the door leading to the bathroom. I was at my house, my hideaway, which meant that Frank must have brought me here. He was the only other person who knew about this house. I tried to sit up, but that made the pain worse, so I lifted my head, looking around, and that's when I realized there was a body next to me.

I swear my ass got happy as hell when I realized it was Rain. Shit, at this point she was the only person I wanted to see, and the fact that she was here next to me made the pain I was feeling irrelevant. I lifted my right arm and reached across my chest so that I could touch her face, and when my fingers made contact with her skin, her eyes popped open and she sat up.

I couldn't see her face because the room was so dark, but I could feel her energy.

"Thee, don't move, let me get the nurse." I grabbed her hand and shook my head to tell her no. I must have had some shit down my throat because I couldn't talk.

"Theory, please let me go get the nurse," she pleaded, but I shook my head to tell her no again, and held on tighter to her hand. I slowly lifted my arm and held it out so that she would lay with me. I didn't want to see a nurse or whoever else was here, I just wanted to feel her body next to mine. My ass was alive and all I wanted was to feel her next to me.

Rain being Rain, hesitated for as long as she could, but then eventually moved close to me. She laid her head on my shoulder and I let my arm fall around her waist. My body hurt like hell, but I didn't care. It only took a minute for my eyes to get heavy again, and I knew I was about to be out, so I didn't fight it.

"Rain, wake up, ma. They need to change his bandages." I opened my eyes when I heard Frank's voice fill the room. His voice was so heavy that even though I could tell he was trying to whisper, he was loud as fuck, and it made me want to laugh, but I couldn't with all the shit they had on me. The pain was worse now, so my body flinched when Rain shifted her weight to move away from me. She felt it and her face showed it.

"I'm sorry," she said, as she scooted toward the side of the bed were Frank was standing. Her words made Frank look at me, and a smile crept across his face along with the look of relief, when his eyes met mine. I guess he was happy I was alive, too.

"How long he been up?" he asked Rain, as he moved to the door, waved his hand in the air, and then walked to the opposite side of the bed.

"Next time your ass decides to catch a few hot ones, can you check Brooks' tee times first? You know his ass is charging us extra because he was on the golf course when I called."

I just shook my head, which for some reason, my neck hurt like hell, too. But then I quickly remembered that I got hit in the shoulder, so the muscle had to be tight from the injury.

I looked past Frank at the nurse who entered the room and when she was next to Frank, he stepped out the way to let her do whatever she was there to do.

"He's awake now, does he still need that?" Rain asked her, pointing to my face, and I assumed she was talking about the tubes and shit around my nose and down my throat. I hoped like hell the nurse said no because it was uncomfortable as hell, and I couldn't wait to feel Rain's lips. Three holes in my body, in pain like a muthafucker, and all I wanted was a damn kiss.

"No, we'll take those out in a minute, but his wounds are bleeding so I need to change these bandages. You might want to step out for a minute…" Before she could finish, Rain was shutting that down.

"I'm staying, do whatever you need to do."

Frank chucked. "I'll be right back, Thee. Try not to die while I'm gone."

I knew Frank well; that was his way of dealing with the fact that I was okay. He had never been the emotional type, so his jokes meant that he was good.

Rain stepped back and watched as the nurse did her thing. I thought she was going to slap her ass a few times from the way that she was handling me, but I guess the nurse's only concern was that my wounds were covered and I was healing properly. I had my teeth clenched the entire time she yanked on my body and inspected my wounds, because that shit hurt like a bitch. Especially when she had to pull me to a seated position to check the one on my back and shoulder. I wasn't soft by any means, but she had a nigga wanting to shed a few tears and on everything, I had to fight like hell not to let them fall.

Once she was done, she did as Rain asked and removed the tube from my nose and out of my throat, and I was happy as hell because that shit had me feeling confined. Not long after the nurse was done, Brooks showed up to check on everything. He had to add more stitches to my side, but all in all he was impressed and amazed that I was even alive. Rain got pissed that he said that, and I had to calm her down to stop her from going in on him.

Now everyone was gone and it was just the two of us, for a minute. I was stuck in this damn bed, supposedly for a minimum of two weeks, which I knew wasn't happening. I had to figure out who the hell shot, me and I couldn't do that from this damn bed. But, at least Rain was with me, so I was content... for a minute anyway.

I was laying there waiting for her to finish her shower so that we could chill for a minute alone, and my mind was moving at lightning speed. I kept trying to figure out if I missed anything, and if anyone stood out to me. Nothing was adding up. There was always somebody who had beef with us, but those niggas knew better than to come at either one of us, guns blazing. The fucked up part about it was I was getting out, so it wasn't like I was a threat. I mean, I was always going to be connected, that was just how that shit worked, but I wasn't a threat if I wasn't right in the middle of everything. So now shouldn't have been the time for anybody to be gunning for me. That was the part that just didn't add up, so I couldn't connect anything to make sense of it.

When I heard a knock on the door, I looked up and nodded for Frank to enter.

"I've got people outside watching the house and before you say shit, I know you can handle your own, but right now your ass can't get out that bed, so I'm not taking any chances."

His expression was serious as hell because he knew me, and he knew I was going to object to the babysitters he was leaving me with.

"You better be glad I can't get out this damn bed while you trying to handle me and shit," I said with a grin.

"Yeah, well for now you don't have a choice, but on another note, we need to discuss what happened," Frank said.

I glanced at the bathroom door and could still hear the shower running, so I figured we were good for a minute.

"Aight, but make it quick. I don't really want to discuss this shit around Rain," I said, nodding towards the bathroom door.

Frank's hand went across his forehead, and his expression hardened before he began. "I know you don't want to hear this shit, but Niles had a hand in this." Frank stood there waiting.

"Come on Frank, Niles is our boy, why the fuck would he want me dead?"

"The fuck if I know, but he's in this shit, Thee. From the time we pulled up on you, he was all over Rain for details about what went down. Like to the point where he was obsessed with it."

"All over Rain?" Out of all the stuff he said, that was the one thing that struck a nerve.

Realizing what he said, Frank clarified. "Not like that. Just grilling her and shit, but the one thing that kept fucking with me was the fact that he slipped up and asked her if she saw the two shooters' faces. How the fuck would he know there were two shooters, unless he had something to do with it? On top of that, he kept asking her if she saw their faces. Why was he so concerned with whether or not she saw their faces? That nigga is up to something, Thee. I don't know why, but I swear on everything, as soon as I figure it out his ass is going six feet."

I lifted my hand and let it slide down my face. I was hearing every word that left Frank's mouth, but for some reason it was like I couldn't really process what he was saying. Was he really telling me that my dude was responsible for me almost dying? As much as I didn't want to believe it, because Niles was my dude, the side of me that never trusted, was going off the charts with doubt.

"Don't make any moves yet," was all I said.

Frank's expression was cold. I could see his need to handle the situation, but he respected me enough to honor my request, no matter how much it was fucking with him.

"He doesn't know shit; in fact, he thinks you're gone. That will only buy us a few days before I have to tell him otherwise, but Thee, I'm telling you… Niles is a dead man walking."

We both glanced at the door when we heard the shower shut off, and the conversation was over.

"I'm out. I'll hit you later if I figure out anything. Brooks said you're here for two weeks. I don't know if we can sit on this for that long."

I nodded understanding completely, but I already knew that. Even before Frank let me know about Niles, I had my mind made up that I wasn't spending two weeks in this damn bed, but now, oh hell no.

Without another word, Frank left the room, pulling the door closed behind him. I sat there processing everything, until Rain came walking out the bathroom dressed in some little ass shorts and one of my V-necks. Her hair was wet and it fell around her face in huge spirals, and the second her eyes met mine, for the first time since I had been awake, I saw the relief that came from knowing that I was okay.

This was my life, and not that being shot wasn't a big deal, but I knew that it was a part of this life. Every day that I walked out my door was another day that I possibly wouldn't make it back. Things like that never really bothered me because I knew I would die one day. I wasn't sitting around waiting on it, but I also didn't walk around with the fear of what-ifs, however, seeing the look on Rain's face let me know that she did. Rain's mind was filled with what-ifs and I had to understand what that was doing to her.

"Come talk to me." I lifted my arm signaling for Rain to join me on the bed. She looked at me, innocence mixed with hesitation, but she walked over to me and sat on the side of the bed. It hurt like hell, but I pulled her into my side and kissed her on the forehead.

"Talk to me Rain, I know you have a lot on your mind."

"I'm fine Thee, I'm just worried about you." Rain was just as much a part of me as I was myself, so I knew her and I knew that she wasn't fine.

"I'm good, you know that, right?"

She tilted her head up just enough to see my face, before she nodded. "You better be. I don't work without you."

My hands glided up and down her arm, taking in the silky feel of her skin. Every time I touched her body, it felt like home. Like I knew exactly where I belonged. I missed that feeling when she was gone. The perfection of the connection we shared was something that people searched their whole lives for, and we had that shit.

"You know what's strange?" I looked down at Rain while my fingers massaged her scalp.

"What's that?" I grinned and stole a kiss from her pouty lips, before I continued.

"I kept hearing that in my head the whole time. It's was like I was there, but I wasn't there. I could hear Brooks in the room. I even think I remember Frank talking, but the one thing that I kept focusing on was your voice telling me that you didn't work without me. I swear I even felt you kiss me."

I knew my ass had to be hallucinating, dreaming, or some shit like that, but it felt so real. I stayed focused on Rain's voice because her words kept racing through my mind. I couldn't sense or feel anything else, but her.

"I told you that," she looked at me and smiled.

"Told me what?"

"That I didn't work without you. Brooks kept saying it didn't look good and how bad the wounds were, so I whispered that in your ear and I kissed you too, right before I told Brooks that you better not die."

Her face got serious which made me laugh. I was laid out with holes in my body, and her little ass was bossing up on the Brooks, threatening him and shit. That's my Autumn Rain.

"So, you had Brooks under pressure? I'm glad his ass is good at what he does."

"Yeah, well not as glad as he is, I bet. I was serious and I made that very clear." Rain sat up slowly, pecked me on the lips, and then slid off the side of the bed. Her shorts were high on her ass, so she pulled them down to cover it, again. Damn, I wanted to fuck her and my dick was a clear indication that part of me was ready and willing, but the other half of my body was not having that shit in no type of way. Oh well, it was coming soon, trust me.

"Are you hungry?" she asked, as she moved across the room and lifted her bag. She placed it on the foot of the bed and pulled out a big ass purple comb and began raking it through her hair.

"Depends on what you're offering," I said, with a smirk.

She rolled her eyes at me before she reached in the bag again and pulled out an elastic tie that she used to fix her hair into a ponytail. When she was done, she returned her bag to its original spot and then climbed on the bed. She stopped on the side of the bed opposite of me, and crossed her legs.

"The fuck you sitting over there for?" I asked.

"Didn't Brooks just have to fix your stitches because you were doing too much?" she said, with a slight frown. I could see the concern in her expression.

"Well Brooks is not here and you're not a damn doctor, so I'm calling the shots right now. I almost died, the least you can do is come lay next to me."

Again, she frowned. "Yeah, well I'm not really anything right now."

Rain crawled slowly over to me and positioned her body next to mine. With everything going on, I had completely forgotten about the fact that Lani's hoe ass got her father to fire Rain. That was another reason why I needed to get my ass out of this bed. Two weeks just wasn't happening.

I kissed Rain on the top of her head. "Don't sweat that. I promise you will get your job back, and the person who did this shit will have to answer to me, trust that."

"You can't make that promise. I don't even know this guy, so how can you make him give me my job back?" I could hear the disappointment mixed with anger in her voice, and that had me wanting to hop my ass out of this bed and go fuck Lani up, and then shoot her bitch ass father. Money made people feel superior, like they could just fuck with peoples' lives without reason. I hated that shit, but street code gave me the right to handle people like that by giving them reality checks, and that was exactly what I had planned for Lani and her father.

"You know me right?" I asked.

Rain tilted her head back just a little so that she could look up at me.

"Yes, Thee, I know you but—"

"No buts, baby girl. If I say its handled, then it's handled. I got you, so all I need you to focus on right now, is me. I need some extra attention." This time when Rain looked up at me, she had a grin on her face, but she playfully rolled her eyes.

"The only extra attention you get right now is me making sure you do what Brooks said, and that means you doing absolutely nothing."

I laughed because she was serious as hell. "So it's like that? I'm just saying Rain, there ain't a damn thing wrong with this half of my body." I held my hand at my waist and waved towards the lower half of my body.

She just shook her head and picked up the remote that was lying next to her, to turn the TV on. Rain was stubborn as hell, so I knew there wasn't shit happening. I was good with that though; as long as she was here with me, I was good… for now. But trust, as soon as I could, I was making up for lost time.

Rain was deep into some movie, so I closed my eyes thinking about everything that was going on. I was mad as hell at the bullshit that Lani pulled and I wanted to tell Rain, but then again, I knew if she found out, she was going straight for Lani. Unfortunately, right now I couldn't stop her, so I had to sit on it.

I had too much shit going on. Lani and her bullshit, on top of the fact that Niles might be the reason for me getting shot, had my head all types of fucked up. I knew one thing for sure and that was that I had to get a hand on things, real quick.

-3-

Rain

"Aye boo." Diamond threw her arms around me the second I opened the door. After I released her, I looked past her into Theory's driveway and across the street, and immediately spotted the vehicles that housed men that were set up to make sure we were protected.

"I know, it's crazy, right?" Diamond said, when she followed the direction of my eyes.

"It's just weird, but this is me now so I better get used to it." I let out a short sigh before I shut and locked the door.

"Frank said that your boy wasn't feeling the guards—he called them babysitters, but since he couldn't stop Frank then he had to suck it up and deal with it," Diamond said with a smirk as she followed me into the living room.

"Trust me, I know. I've heard it more than enough. He's so damn arrogant that the idea of somebody doing something for him that he feels like he can do for himself, is pissing him off."

"So, how is he? I mean, Frank said he's good, but he did get shot three times." Diamond sat down on the sofa and I was right next to her.

"He's good, I guess. He sent the nurse home this morning and told her not to come back. He won't take the pain meds they gave him so I know he's hurting, but he acts like he's fine. It's only been four days and his foolish self thinks he's about to get out this house."

Diamond laughed. "Girl, you have the ultimate alpha male. That man is not about to be laid up in this house and you know it. I'm sure if it were up to him, he would have been up and out the next day."

"Girl, trust me, I know. No matter how much I complain, he keeps making it clear that he will not be hiding."

"How 'bout this, I know he's working on limited energy, so every time he tries to make moves, just give him some and wipe his ass out."

I looked at Diamond and laughed. "Girl stop, I'm not going there with you, but trust me, I thought about it."

"See, problem solved. You know he won't turn you down," Diamond shrugged.

"So, what's up with you. I see you're pretty cozy with Frank?"

"Yeah, we're good. I haven't really seen much of him though, because of all this. He's stressed and he won't talk about it. He stayed with me last night, but I swear he didn't sleep at all. So what's the deal anyway? I know you had to be freaking out."

"I don't really know because it kind of all happened so fast. A car pulled up and bullets started flying. Thee used his body to cover mine, which is how he got hit so many times. I didn't really see anything until it was over, but Frank thinks Niles has something to do with it, and I do too."

Diamond looked at me with her eyebrows raised. "Niles, Niles…as in their homeboy Niles?"

I nodded and continued. "He was just acting real strange about the whole thing. He didn't even really seem concerned about Thee. He just kept grilling me about what I saw and if I saw their faces, but get this… he asked me if I saw the two shooters' faces."

Diamond looked at me confused for a second and then it clicked. "So he knew how many?"

"Exactly."

"Did you tell them; do they know?"

"I haven't really talked to Thee about it, but I'm guessing Frank told him, so I'm sure Thee knows by now."

"Damn, that's messed up. I wonder why he would do that. I mean, I don't really know them that well, but it seemed like they were pretty solid."

"Yeah, I know, that's what I thought, but I guess not."

"What's up Diamond, my boy with you?" Theory turned the corner to enter the living room, moving slow. I could see the pain written all over his face in every step he took, but I knew there was no point in me mentioning it.

"Nah, he's running the streets, probably chasing after some whorish ass female," Diamond smiled at Theory.

He laughed and then grabbed his side. "Don't trip. If he's in the streets he's handling business, trust that."

"Like I'm going to believe you. Hell, I know how that goes. You'll lie for him."

"Just like you'll lie for her," he said, as I stood to move next to him.

"True, but the difference is that she wouldn't put me in the position to have to lie for her," Diamond said with a smug grin, and then winked at me.

"What the fuck ever," Theory laughed, before he leaned down and kissed me on the cheek.

"I'm about to get in the shower real quick, so I'll needed you in a minute to redo these bandages."

"I'm heading out anyway," Diamond said, after she was on her feet.

"You don't have to leave ma, it will only take her a minute," Theory said. I knew he was just trying to keep Diamond around so that I wouldn't be stressing him about the fact that he was up, moving around.

"Yeah, stay. I need you to tell me what's been up at work." I frowned, remembering that I no longer had a job.

Diamond looked at me like she smelled something sour. "Bullshit is what's been up. I miss you. They gave me Hanson for my last shoot and he can't do shit right, oh my God. Don't even get me started," Diamond said, with frustration before she fell back into the sofa.

I laughed, but then caught Thee out of the corner of my eye and he had a weird look on his face.

"Aight, I'm about to go handle this shower. I'll call you when I'm ready." He kissed me on the cheek and started moving slowly towards the back of the house.

I watched until he was out of sight and then joined Diamond on the sofa; she was staring at me with a goofy ass grin.

"What hoe?" I laughed, because I knew why she was looking at me like that.

"Do I get to pick my own dress?" she said, and then laughed.

"Just for that, no, but I'm not getting married anytime soon, so don't even go there," I said, rolling my eyes.

"Girl please, you love that man and he loves you more. Y'all cute though. Maybe I'll make up my damn mind and pick a lane one day," she laughed.

"Does it even work like that?" I asked.

"I like what I like and right now, that's Frank. That man has given me a newfound respect for dick." Diamond burst out laughing right after she finished her sentence.

"You so damn stupid. I swear, I can't deal with you."

"I'm serious, but we'll save that for another time."

Diamond spent the next hour filling me in on everything that I missed over the past few days at work, and it had me all in my feelings. I loved me job. I worked hard to get it and it infuriated me that one person could just take that away from me, without even once seeing my face, or having a conversation with me. It just didn't make sense, but I was determined to get to the bottom of it, and real soon. Right now, I had to focus on Theory because I knew that his mind was made up about leaving this house, and he could barely manage to walk from one end of it to the other.

After Diamond left and I made it back to the bedroom, I found exactly what I didn't want to see. Theory was dressed from the waist down in jeans, which meant that he had intentions of leaving the house.

"Stop looking at me like that. You already knew I wasn't about to sit my ass up in this house for two weeks. I have shit to figure out and I can't do that laying up in that bed."

I didn't say a word because I was pissed and knew it wouldn't matter anyway. I simply walked into the bathroom to get his supplies so that I could re-bandage his wounds. Of course, he was right behind me, but he didn't speak, either. Theory just stood in front of the mirror, lowering his hands on the marble counter, leaning forward slightly to get ready for me to cover his wounds.

As I worked, I could see him watching me through the mirror, but he kept quiet until I reached his left shoulder to cover the last one. I stared at it for a minute, because the gunshot hit right in the area where my name was. After a few seconds of reflection, I lifted the bandage and began to cover it again, with a clean one. When I was done, he turned to face me, leaning against the counter, with his hands placed on it, one on each side.

"I'll get another one," he said randomly, as I cleaned up after myself, placing a few items in the trash before I looked up at him.

"It's fine."

He laughed under his breath and waited for me to be near him again, before he reached for me and slowly moved me into his personal space. He flinched and his jaw tightened, but he was so too damn stubborn to admit that he was in pain.

Theory used one hand to hold me in place while he let the other grip my neck. "You mad at me?"

He wore a smirk because he knew I was upset, simply by the fact that I wasn't talking to him. I just looked into his eyes with a hard stare, but still didn't say a word, which made him laugh.

"Rain, open your damn mouth," he said, with that stupid ass grin that immediately had me wanting to smile right back at him.

"I'm not mad at you, I'm just worried."

"I don't need you to worry about me Rain." Theory's expression turned serious as he looked into my eyes.

"How can you even say that? You got shot three times, you can barely move without killing yourself, and you're about to leave here to go do God knows what. Yeah okay, I won't worry about you. That's just dumb, right?"

"Chill with all that. That's not what I mean and you know it. What I'm saying is this is my life; this is how shit works. I know we haven't really had a conversation about that yet, and we will real soon, but you know who I am. I can't just sit here and do nothing. If I don't get out there now and figure this shit out, it's only going to get worse. It's not just me anymore. If somebody's coming for me, then that means they're coming for you too, and you know I'm not having that shit. I need to be making moves, Rain."

I knew he was right. I wasn't one-hundred percent sure about every detail of his life, but I knew enough to know that whoever did this needed to be handled, and Theory wasn't going to rest mentally or physically until that happened.

"You can't ask me not to worry. Just like you want me to respect the fact that you have to go do whatever, then you have to respect the fact that I'm going to worry about you while you're out there doing it."

Theory's expression softened just a little, before a smirk formed. "That sounds like love, Autumn Rain. You love me?"

I rolled my eyes, but couldn't hide my smile. "I like you a little bit, sometimes, but not right now though."

Theory laughed and leaned down to kiss me. When he released it, his expression changed and I could tell that he had something heavy on his mind, because just that quickly his mood turned sour. He nudged me just a little to get me to move away from him, before he caught my hand and led me back to the bedroom.

"Sit down, I need to talk to you about something." Now he really had me worried. I sat on the foot of the bed and he was a few feet away, standing in front of me. I could see the tension in his body as he began to speak.

"I know why you lost your job." He watched my expression and waited.

"What do you mean you know why; do you know the guy?"

"I know who he is, but more importantly, I know his daughter," Theory said, and then again he waited.

You have to be fucking kidding me. I know he was not about to tell me that I lost my job because of one of his bitches.

"So, I guess I should feel honored that the reason I lost my job is because you stopped fucking some bitch that wasn't ready to let go. You did it for me, right?"

I knew I sounded crazy, but I was pissed. My job was important to me. I loved my job and to know that some spiteful bitch called in a favor to daddy, just because Theory was holding out on her, made it even worse.

Theory laughed, which didn't help, but he quickly got it together when he saw the look on my face based on his reaction.

"It's fucked up and I know it, but trust me, I'll fix it. When I told you I would take care of it, I meant it."

"Yeah, well, you better. It's my job Theory. You might not get it, but that meant a lot to me." I jumped up thinking I was about to storm out of the room, but he stopped me by stepping in front of me.

"Calm the fuck down and you can chill with all that slick shit. I know it's important to you, which is why I said I'm going to fix it. I can't help her dumb ass don't understand simple shit like the fact that I'm not fucking with her anymore, but don't come at me like I'm the one who fired your ass. You think I wanted that? I know how much you love what you do, Rain."

"And don't you sit here and act like I don't have the right to be mad about it," I yelled back.

"You can be mad all you want, fuck shit up for all I care, but I better not be the focus of that shit." I felt his voice vibrating through my body as he spoke. There was so much authority in his delivery that I had to hide my smile. His arrogant ass was sexy as hell, the way he called himself handling me.

I stood there just looking at him, while he glared back with his eyes narrowed, arms folded and legs shoulder width apart. His stance and body language said more than his words.

"And I don't give a fuck about you standing there pouting either, you know I'm right and you know this shit is not my fault. You want me to go fuck the bitch to get your job back I will, but we both know that ain't what you want, so like I said, calm all that down and let me handle it. You will get your job back and I promise you that."

"You probably want to fuck her anyway," I mumbled before I tried to turn away from him, but he caught my arm and stepped towards my body, looking down at me like he wanted to take my head off.

"The only person I want to fuck is you, and since I can't do that right now then I guess we'll both have to deal with it. But, trust me, it's coming, and that will put an end to that funky little attitude you got right now." His expression was hard for a few seconds before a smile crept through. And then, he leaned down and kissed me, but I refused to kiss him back, no matter how bad I wanted to, which made him laugh.

"Yeah, aight, trust me, I got something for that," he said, and stepped around me to walk into his closet. I followed behind him and stood in the door, watching him eyeing the racks of clothes that lined his closet walls.

"Who is she?" I asked, noticing that he never said.

He lifted a sweatshirt and then turned to look at me. "Lani."

It took me a minute before it clicked. "That's that bitch that—"

Theory pointed at me and looked me right in my eyes. "Don't start. I said I'll take care of it, and you already know there ain't shit there other than the fact that she's pissed because she's not you."

I held my tongue and watched as he struggled to pull the sweatshirt in his hands over his head, and then picked up a box that held a pair of Timbs.

I left the closet and started going through my things so that I could get dressed. If he was leaving, I wasn't about to sit up in this house alone all day.

"The fuck you think you're going?" he asked, when he realized what I was doing.

"Home, I need to get more clothes and I'm not about to sit in this house all day by myself. I may not have a job, but I do still have a life." I was still slightly pissed that his past cost me my job, so I threw that out there.

He shook his head, choosing to ignore that. "Let me see who Frank has out there and I'll get them to take you. I can't trust you out there by yourself right now, until I figure out what's going on."

I frowned, I was not about to be stuck with some guy I didn't know all day, or even worse, until he had this so called handled.

"Thee, I'll be fine."

"I'm not about to argue with you about this. Just for today, okay? After I see what's what, then we'll talk."

He walked past me and started collecting his things from the dresser where I had placed them after Frank gave them to me, when we first got Theory to the house. I knew the conversation was over, so I just let it go and prepared to get dressed so that I could meet my babysitter. Being with Theory meant changes and it was going to take some adjusting, but there was no other option; his life was my life, so it was what it was.

-4-

Theory

This house was off the radar and I was never really here a lot, but I kept two cars here, just in case. So, after I got Rain set up with Bull and laid out her plans with him, I headed to the garage so that I could leave. I had a lot a shit to do and half the day was already gone. Once I backed out of the driveway and hit my street, I glanced at the two trucks set up that were watching my spot. The crew inside offered a head nod as I passed them, but stayed put.

I was still laughing to myself at the way that Rain was pouting when I left her with Bull. Her face was all kinds of screwed up when she looked him over, and that shit was funny as hell. Bull was about three hundred pounds and never smiled. His ass always looked angry about something, but fuck it. I wasn't about to have her around some nigga who she might actually find attractive. Bull was married with kids, which still bugged me out because his ass was mean as fuck, so I couldn't for the life of me, figure out how he was able to convince anyone to marry him. I knew Bull would keep her safe, but would also respect the fact that she was off limits. I trusted Rain, but I knew that a man was going to be a man, so she wasn't about to be up in just any nigga's face.

I hated that the second she was back in my life, shit just got out of hand and went completely left. Here I was trying to wrap my mind around getting out, but niggas wanna do dumb shit and force my hand. I didn't take that lightly, and whoever was behind this was about to pay in the worst way. The fucked up part was that I had a gut feeling that Niles had something to do with this. After Frank hit me up with details about the day I was shot and other odd things that Niles had been doing leading up to this, it just made sense, and that was fucking with me. But, it was going to be dealt with, but first, I was about to pay Lani's dumb ass a visit. She had royally fucked up and was about to deal with the consequences.

When I pulled up at Lani's house, I instantly got pissed and prayed that she hadn't changed the security code to the gate that circled her property. Once I keyed the code she had given me almost a year ago and the gate opened, I smiled, but that was short lived. The second I hit the circular drive, I noticed Savannah's truck, which I knew very well because my crew had hooked her up. I had to admit it was nice as hell, but seeing it meant that she was here and that meant that I was about to have to deal with double the bullshit.

I sat there for a minute to get my bearings before I could find the energy to get out of my car. Hell, I had been shot and laid up for the past few days, and I could feel it in every inch of my body, but, I needed things to be handled, so here I was.

After I reached the front door, I tried the handle and of course, it opened. Her dumb ass never locked the damn door. I guess she thought that security gate meant something, but if somebody really wanted to get to her, all they had to do was climb it or cut through the shit, and then they could walk right into her house.

The second I was inside, I heard laughing coming from the kitchen, so I yelled her name. A brother was still in pain, so no need to do more than I had to. A few minutes later, she appeared looking mad at the world, with Savannah right behind her.

"I'm not getting that bitch her job back, so I don't know why you're here," Lani said with an evil smirk, as she moved my way, stopping a few feet away from me.

I laughed, sarcastically. "Are you really that fucking stupid? Trust me, you will."

"I don't know what makes you think that, but you and that bitch can kiss my ass," Lani said, and I could tell that she was more hurt, than angry. She knew from the first time that she saw Rain's name on me and asked about her that she would never replace her. I made that clear and back then, I didn't even know if I would ever see Rain again, but I did know that no woman would ever take her place. Savannah snickered, which made me glance at her, but she looked away.

"I don't think that, I know that, and you know me well enough to understand what that means," I said, which made Savannah suck her teeth.

"And you need to chill with all that. In fact, this don't have shit to do with you, so you can run along. I know there's a dick somewhere that's waiting to be sucked," I said, pointing at Savannah, causing her to give me the most hateful stare.

"Fuck you, Theory. She's my best friend, so it has everything to do with me. I told her you weren't shit from day one, and now she finally sees why."

This bitch was tripping. "So she's your best friend now. Was she your best friend when I had you bent over my desk?" I asked, looking right at Lani. Fuck them both. At this point, I didn't care.

Lani looked at me like she wanted to cry, before her eyes fell on Savannah. Savannah didn't have a chance to say anything before Lani smacked the shit out of her. Savannah grabbed her face, looking shocked.

"Don't act like you didn't know. I'm not the only one he slept with and you know that," Savannah yelled, through the tears that were falling because of the contact that Lani made with her face.

"But, you're supposed to be my best friend; that should have meant something."

"Yo, I don't give a fuck about any of that. Y'all can argue about that shit later." I stepped to Lani and grabbed a hand full of her hair before she could move away from me. I brought her close to my face and it took every ounce of energy I had to maintain.

"You are going to go to your father and get her job back. Don't forget, I know shit about you and him that I'm sure the world would love to know. Fix this shit."

Savannah's eyes fell on us, but she knew better than to try to help Lani.

"I don't care what you know, it's not going to make me get that bitch her job back."

I laughed, sarcastically and shoved her away from me, before I turned to walk to the door.

I stopped just before I left. "Get her job back and stay the fuck away from her, or I will ruin your ass. I'm sure the world would love to see daddy's little princess, sucking dick and snorting cocaine."

I looked back at Lani and her mouth fell open before I walked out of her front door. She didn't say a word, because she knew she had fucked up. Lani was your typical spoiled rich kid, whose parents paid her a lot of money and very little attention. She was wild and reckless, which didn't really matter to me because she wasn't my girl. I was sure she had forgotten all about the videos we made. I always kept them, just in case her father tried to come at me with some bullshit. I knew how men like him worked, and they played dirty.

I also knew for a fact that her father was sleeping with a bunch of under aged girls. Frank caught him one night at one of his events, and because Frank thinks like me, he caught it on video. Frank questioned the girl later and found out she was sixteen, and the family member of one of Loyalty's artists. She admitted that he threatened her into sex by saying that her cousin would lose her record deal, if she didn't. We sent someone to handle him about the situation, and delivered a message that if we found out he was still up to no good, then the world would find out, and as insurance, we kept the video. I learned early in life to never show your hand until it was absolutely necessary, and right now was that time. I knew that Rain would have her job back real soon and from here on out, would be untouchable. Detroit valued his image too much to fuck with me.

Now that that was handled, I needed to meet up with Frank to find out what the deal was with Niles. I just planned on popping up on Niles first for confirmation. I had a feeling that Frank and I were about to be splitting our profits two ways, instead of three.

"You busy?" I could tell my voice startled Niles, but not more than the sight of me standing in his doorway.

"Damn, Thee, I'm glad to see you. Frank told me you were underground for a minute so I didn't expect to see you anytime soon, but damn, I'm glad you're okay," Niles was rambling, as he stood to move towards me. He acted as if he was about to hug me, but I held my hand up to stop him.

"Still sore," I said, with no real expression. I wanted him to sweat. Whether or not he knew I was suspicious of him, I wanted him to be on edge, unable to read me. The idea of not knowing was going to make him reckless and before long, he would tell on himself.

"Yeah, my bad. I didn't really think about that. Shit, your ass got shot three times, four days ago, and you're up moving around. That's some serious shit Theory." Niles offered a half ass smile, but I could see the concern for his future in his eyes. I had a good mind to shoot his dumb ass right now, but I needed to know who he was partnered up with. Even if Niles had a hand in this whole thing, there was no way he was the brains behind it. When it came to our situation, Frank and I put shit together and just handed Niles his duties. Niles was more concerned with money and women to invest any time into using his damn brain.

"Frank said you hit the streets while Brooks was working on me, did you find out anything?" Niles was behind his desk again, but I chose to stand. It was killing me to be on my feet, but I needed the intimidation factor, and towering over Niles made a point.

"This shit is crazy Thee, nobody knows anything. It's like nobody's talking."

"Oh yeah?" I looked Niles right in his eyes and found the answer I was looking for. I had a gut feeling, but there was a small part of me that was hoping that it wasn't true. We had all been through so much; he was supposed to be my dude, but when it was all said and done, money trumped loyalty. Niles loved money so it looked like somebody offered him the right amount to turn on me.

"Yeah, I mean, I've been talking to everybody and nobody seems to want to talk, but don't worry Thee, I promise you, we'll figure this shit out. Nobody comes at us like that, without consequences."

I laughed to myself when he said us; shit, I was the one with three holes in me. The fuck he mean us?

"Aight, well hit me up if you get any leads, I'm heading out." I turned to leave but Niles jumped up and was next to me again.

"I can swing by later and we can go over things," Nile said, and then looked at me to wait for my reaction.

"Nah, I'm good on that. I'll be off the grid for a minute, so just hit me up."

"So, you're not heading back to your crib then?"

This muthafucker. It was taking everything I had not to just light his ass up, but I knew that getting rid of Niles was not going to solve the problem, just yet. I still had to worry about who he was working with, and I needed him alive to figure that out.

I just chuckled and left his office. If he didn't know before, he definitely knew now that I was on to him, and that fear right there was about to make him fuck up. I made my way back into my car with one thought on my mind, and that was that Niles had better get right with God, because his end was coming.

*****

"You should have shot his ass! Fuck him, Thee. We don't need him to find out who he's working with. The streets will eventually talk." Frank peered at me as he paced in front of me. I was at his house and we were in his kitchen.

"Trust me, I thought about it, but we'll sit on it for a minute. He knows, though. I could see it in his eyes. Niles knows he's a dead man walking."

"You're giving his ass time to make moves. What if he runs? You know he's a little bitch, Thee. Fuck that, we're 'bout to go get his ass now." Frank lifted his gun off the counter next to him and started towards the door. He was mad as hell, which made me laugh before I called his name.

"Frank, calm the fuck down and chill. I promise, Niles has a hot one waiting on him, but right now, we wait. He'll get what's coming, I promise." I looked back over my shoulder, but didn't move. Rain was right, even though I would never admit it to her. I didn't have any business out here, and I could feel it in every breath that I took, so I damn sure wasn't about to chase Frank's angry ass, unless I had to.

He stood there for a minute with his hands against his hips, looking down, and then at me, as if he were trying to decide his next move. Eventually, he walked back into the kitchen and placed his gun back on the counter.

"Soon Thee. We take care of this real soon and I can't promise that I won't off his ass if I see him anytime soon, so don't expect that."

I just laughed. If ever I claimed anyone as family, Frank was it. I had always been on the fence with Niles, but I never had doubts about Frank. That meant a lot coming from me because I didn't trust anyone worth shit.

"I feel you, just stay your ass away from him for now. Put some people on him and see what moves he's making. Let them report to me, so that your hostile ass won't kill him before we're ready."

Frank looked at me like he could shoot me for saying that. "Yeah, aight, just know that we need this handled soon. My patience is gone."

"The fuck you mean gone, you know your ass ain't never had no damn patience in the first place."

Frank shook his head and walked over to the cabinet. A few minutes later, he had a bottle of Hennessey in his hand and two glasses. He set one in front of me before he got comfortable in the chair across from me.

"I know you need this shit because you sitting there looking like you wanna cry. Rain told me you won't take the pain meds Brooks left for you."

"Hell, I need that whole bottle and even then I don't think that will touch this shit I'm feeling. Every inch of my body is in pain."

"That's your damn fault. You know your ass should be laid up right now." Frank filled both of our glasses and I downed mine, literally, in one run before I refilled it.

"Yeah, well this shit ain't gonna figure itself out, so it's not like I really had a choice, did I?"

Frank lifted his glass and nodded.

"I saw your girl today." I thought about the fact that Diamond showed up at my place today which meant that Frank had to be the one to tell her.

He finished his drink and then refilled his glass, all while trying to hold onto the smile that was creeping through.

"We're chilling," Frank said, with a smirk.

"Aye, do what you do, bruh." I liked Diamond and as far as I was concerned, she had to be alright because Rain was fucking with her strong and Rain didn't deal with people. She was never the kind to have so-called friends. She was cool with people, but never let them get close to her.

"We'll see how it goes, but for now, I'm just chilling."

I just laughed. Frank had women—hell, we all did, but Frank was the most like me. He wanted that one person in his corner.

"She the one?" I lifted my glass and looked right at Frank. I could see him thinking about it.

"If I'm what she wants," Frank said.

"Hell, she chilling, right? You're obviously what she wants."

"Nah, not like that. Her last relationship was with another female."

That caught my attention. "Word?"

"Hell, yeah."

I laughed. "That shit might work in your favor."

"Fuck you, Thee. That shit is cool when you're just chilling, but why the fuck would I wanna wife someone who can't pick a damn lane."

Frank looked serious as hell. "Wife? Damn, it's like that?"

I could see it all over his face. He was feeling Diamond, but stressing over her past.

"Not like that, I'm just saying. I'm feeling her so for now it is what it is," Frank said.

"I feel you," I said, leaning back to get my phone out my pocket. I knew it was Rain before I even looked at it.

"So, you really going to stay out all day?" Rain said, as soon as I answered.

I chuckled. "Well, hello to you, too."

"Don't play, Thee. Where are you and when are you coming back?"

"I'm at Frank's, where are you?"

"I'm on my way back to the house."

"I'm heading that way in a minute," I lied, knowing I was about to kick it with Frank for a while longer.

"Don't make me come get you," Rain snapped, which made me laugh.

"You do know that you can't do shit, unless I say so, because if I call Bull and tell him to take your ass straight to the house and not to let you leave, that's how it's going down."

"And by the way, next time you decided to provide me with an escort, can you at least make sure he speaks. This guy is creepy as hell. I don't think he's said two words since you left."

"His job is to make sure you're safe, not to make a damn social connection. You want to talk to somebody, call me," I said, in all seriousness. There wasn't shit she needed to say to him anyway.

"Oh my God, I can't with you. Just hurry up and get here."

She was frustrated as hell and it made me laugh. "You miss me Autumn Rain?"

"No, I'm just ready to get rid of Mr. Creepy Town," she said firmly, and then hung up.

I thought about calling her back, but decided to wait. I had something for her smart ass mouth later. I didn't care if I busted every stitch I had in my body, I planned on being inside Rain tonight, well, that was if my body cooperated with me.

"Who she with?" Frank asked, snapping me out of my thoughts about Rain.

I chuckled. "Bull."

"Damn, Thee, that's cold. You know his ass scary as fuck. I'm still trying to figure out how his ass has a wife and kids."

"Shit, me too. It was either Bull or Rick, and I didn't wanna have to fuck around and shoot Rick for trying me. He be on his shit, but that muthafucker thinks he's a pimp."

Frank laughed. "Rick ain't stupid and he knows you're not playing with a full deck."

"Shit, you never know. Look at this bullshit with Niles."

"Yeah, you're right," Frank said, nodding before he finished off the last of his drink.

We kicked it for a little while longer before I found the energy to get my ass up and head home. I was done for the day and ready to chill with Rain, even though I knew she was going in on me, first, for leaving her with Bull and being gone all day. It didn't matter though; as long as she was safe, I was good. She could be mad all she wanted, but I was always gonna do what was necessary to keep her safe.

Rain

I looked at my phone and my mom was calling. I hadn't talked to her in over a month and I actually missed her. I had a good relationship with my adoptive parents and even though they weren't thrilled about me taking the job at *Urban Pride,* they dealt with it. They both knew that Theory was the reason behind my move and as much as they didn't like it, they knew that there wasn't anything they could do to stop it. It was like deep inside, they always knew that I would find my way back to him.

"Are you hiding from us Rain?" I could hear the smile in her voice, but I also knew that she was partially serious.

"No, Ma. I've just been busy." She would call at the exact time I was in a drive-by and lost my job.

"Well, we miss you. Your father mentioned flying there to look for you if I didn't get you on the phone soon."

I laughed at the sight of my father jumping on a plane to Atlanta, just to get face time with me. He was that person.

"I miss you too. Maybe I'll fly down and come see you guys soon."

It wasn't like I had anything else to do since I lost my damn job.

"That would be nice, Rain. I'm sure your father would appreciate that. You know how he is. How's Jamel?"

I let out a short sigh. My parents still didn't know about Mel and they damn sure didn't know about Theory. I wasn't ready for that conversation, and now most definitely wasn't the time.

"He's good, Ma. We're just going through some things right now, so I don't know if we'll make it."

"Really? Do you want to talk about it?" my mother asked. She and I didn't see eye to eye on my relationships, but she was secretly pulling for Jamel if it meant that I would let go of the idea of Theory. They didn't even know Theory, but they didn't like him. He was just another street kid who wasn't worth my time. They were grateful for him because honestly, he was the only reason why I survived the way I did, that much they understood, but for some reason, that wasn't enough. He wasn't good enough for me.

"Not really," was all I said.

"Oh, before I forget, your sister's job is transferring her to a location there in Atlanta. Have you heard from her?"

I almost laughed at the thought of me actually talking to Charlotte. She was also adopted from foster care, but had been with our parents from the time she was 10 years old. When I came along, it changed things for her. She was used to being the center of our parents' attention, and then there was me. The crazy thing was that I didn't care about the attention. In fact, most of the time I just wanted to be left alone, but it still seemed like Charlotte hated me for my parents' intentions. She put on a good front for our parents, but all in all, she and I could live the rest of our lives not dealing with each other, and I wouldn't shed a tear.

The funniest part of this whole thing was the fact that my mother was telling me that her job was transferring her to Atlanta. Charlotte was a stripper, that much I knew, because Mel found out and made a point of telling me. She had been one for years, so I was trying to figure out what job she convinced my parents that she had that was willing to set her up in Atlanta.

"No, I haven't."

I was sure my mother sensed my irritation from her asking me about Charlotte, but I really didn't care. We weren't kids anymore, so there was no need to pretend.

"Rain, don't do that. I know you guys haven't always gotten along, but she's your sister. She loves you. Just call her please," my mother said, sounding disappointed and almost begging.

"Yeah, okay." I agreed only because I didn't want to hurt my mother's feelings, but there was no way in hell I was wasting one second of my time on Charlotte. That just want happening.

"I love you, Rain. Thank you, and please call your father. He really misses you. You girls are breaking his heart because he feels like y'all just threw him away." I knew my mother was only stating how my father really felt and not attempting to make me feel bad, but it still hurt a little.

"I will, Ma. I have to go."

I ended the call and sat on Theory's bed, stuck in my feelings for a minute. Even though I loved my parents, I still struggled with the whole family environment thing. I was truly grateful for them and I knew they loved me unconditionally, but it was still hard for me to connect with their feelings on me being away, or not talking to them every day. I planned on working on that.

I heard the front door and then Theory's voice, along with who I assumed was Bull. Hell, I didn't know what his voice sounded like because he barely said two words to me all day.

A few minutes later, Theory was standing in the doorway of his bedroom, grinning at me.

"I'm home now, you can stop sitting there looking like somebody stole your damn bike."

"Wow, you really do think everything is about you, don't you?" I rolled my eyes as he moved towards me and stopped right before his body made contact with my legs.

"Everything is about me and you know it," he said arrogantly, while he wore a cocky grin that had me wanting to jump up and kiss him.

"Not even close," I said and stood, while he refused to step back, so our bodies were touching. I reached for his sweatshirt and began lifting it to check his bandages and of course, his mind was somewhere else.

"Damn, can I get a hello and a kiss first?" he asked, looking down at me.

"Not even what you're thinking. I just want to see if you're bleeding because your stubborn ass was gone all day, doing God knows what."

Just like I suspected. The bandage on his side was spotted, but not too bad. Theory didn't say anything because he knew I was going to follow it up with something smart.

"Sit down," I said, rolling my eyes again and attempting to step around him, but Theory moved quickly and used his arms to hold me in place. After he kissed me he let me go, struggled to pull his sweat shirt over his head, and then sat on the bed and waited.

The second I was in the bathroom, I heard his voice. "So, your girl swings both ways, huh?" he asked, and I grabbed all of his supplies, tossed them on the bed, and started removing the bandage on his shoulder.

"Yeah, so?" I said.

"So, she's got my boy's head all fucked up."

I looked down at Theory, waiting for him to explain.

"You know he's feeling her. He's just stressing about her switching teams on him." Theory had a grin on his face, looking a little too amused about the situation.

"Well, if he gives her a reason not to then she won't," I said, truthfully. Diamond and I had that conversation a few times.

"Does it even work like that?" Theory asked.

"Hell, I don't know. She just always says she likes what she likes. Right now that's Frank."

"So y'all close?"

I narrowed my eyes at him. "Not that kinda close," I said.

He laughed. "Don't act like that, I'm good with whatever. I just need to know if I you need supervision while you're around her. I don't do that sharing shit with anybody. You're all mine."

Theory grabbed me around the waist then pulled my body in between his legs and looked up at me with a smug grin.

I just shook my head and pulled away from him, to finish removing his bandages.

"Yo, let me hop in the shower before you hook me up and what about dinner? I'm hungry as fuck." I collected his old bandages while he stood to head to the bathroom.

"Do you want me to cook?"

"Yeah, that's cool. I see Frank bought out the damn store and shit."

I laughed, thinking about the fact that Frank paid the nurse to go grocery shopping the first day we were in the house. He had so much stuff in here it was insane, but he told me he didn't know what I liked, so he told her to get everything.

"Alright, well I'm about to go do that."

"Or you can come in here with me," Theory said, with a smirk.

"Or I can go start dinner," I said, and left him standing there and started towards the door, until I heard him behind me.

"You know it's coming. The longer you hold out, the worse it's going to be." He winked at me and then walked into the bathroom. I left the room grinning like a little kid.

*****

The sound of my phone vibrating on the nightstand next to me woke me up, so I pulled away from Theory as slowly as possible, but his reflexes kicked in and he tightened his hold on me, so I shoved him just a little, so that he would let me go.

When I had my phone in my hand, I noticed it was one of the numbers from *Urban Pride,* so I climbed off the side of the bed and left the bedroom before I answered.

"Hello."

"Hey boo, wake up. We have work to do today," Diamond sang into the phone. So, I pulled it away from my face for a second to see what time it was. It was just after eight.

"Please tell me you're calling to say that I have my job back," I said, knowing that Theory mentioned handling Lani before he left yesterday.

"Your job, your office, and two assignments, so get your ass up and get dressed."

"Are you serious?"

"You know I don't play about stuff like that, now get dressed and meet me down here. Dallas was going to call you, but I told him I would. He still needs to talk to you, but you're back, boo."

"Thank God. I was really hoping I wasn't going to have to go handle this myself."

"What's that all about?" Diamond asked. I still hadn't told her that one of Theory's bitches was behind me losing my job.

"Long story. Let me go tell Thee. Give me an hour and I'll be there."

"Hurry up, I miss you. I've been on my own since you left. You know I don't mess with these scandalous hoes around here."

"You need to stop, but let me go so I can get dressed."

"Aight, boo. See you in a few."

I couldn't help, but smile even though I really wanted to fuck that Lani chick up. At least Theory handled it and I had my job back. I would figure out how to deal with her later and trust me, I was laying hands on that hoe as soon as I laid eyes on her.

After I ended my call with Diamond, I damn near skipped back into the bedroom to tell Theory. At first there was so much going on with him being shot and recovering that I didn't get a chance to really miss being at work, but when he left me yesterday, reality set in. I felt out of place like I didn't know what to do with myself.

From the day I took my first photography class my senior year of high school, I fell in love with it. There really wasn't a day that passed where I didn't have my camera in my hands at some point. Then I got the job at *Urban Pride* and could actually see my work in print and online, and there was just something about that. It was a part of me.

I leaned down over Theory and I could tell I startled him, because his hand immediately went to the gun that was resting beside him on the nightstand, but the second he opened his eyes, he relaxed.

"What's wrong?" he mumbled, trying to shake the disoriented state that he was in.

"Nothing, Diamond just called and I guess your little friend made that call to daddy because I got my job back. We have an assignment, so I'm about to get dressed and head out."

"Okay, I'll take you." Theory sat up and I could see the effects of the movement on his face, as his jaw tightened and he grabbed his side.

"I can drive myself, you don't have to. I can just take one of the cars you have here."

"Rain, chill, I can take you. I need to be up anyway."

I let it go because the argument was pointless. I grabbed a few things out of my bag and headed towards the bathroom. I could hear Theory on the phone as I shut the door. After I relived my bladder, washed my hands and brushed my teeth, I climbed into the shower and stood under the water, letting it massage my body. A few minutes later, I heard the toilet flush and water running. Right after that I heard the bathroom door shut, so I finished my shower, and dressed in my panties and bra, before I went back into the room. Theory was in the closet, but I could hear him on the phone, so I grabbed my jeans and stepped into them. Theory was already dressed in a pair of black jeans and holding a dark gray Henley, which he tossed on the bed and then came straight to me.

"Aight, Frank, I'm about to get dressed so that I can drop Rain off. Meet me at the shop. I need to head there and take care of a few things. Yeah, aight." Theory laughed, ended his call, and then tossed his phone on the bed. I was in the process of buckling my jeans, but he stopped me by sliding his hand into them, while kissing my neck.

"Why you let me go to sleep last night Rain?" he asked, in-between kisses on my neck and then my jawline, while his fingers found my center. They moved slowly in and out of me, shutting down any ability I had to think straight. I inhaled deep and then let it go, trying to get my head right, before I grabbed his wrist and backed away from him.

"Because you needed it," I said, moving to the other side of the bed, making sure we had enough distance between us. As much as I wanted to feel him right now, I had to get to work, and if we took it a step further, neither of us was leaving anytime soon.

Theory looked at me with a cocky grin and pointed at me. "Sleep I can do without, but that shit right there I need," he winked at me, and then walked into the bathroom. I was pissed because now the rest of my day was going to be spent thinking about him. Lord, help me make it through this day.

An hour later, Theory pulled up in front of my office and I grabbed my camera bags out the back seat, while he got out to open my door. Once I was on the sidewalk, I pulled my bag up on my shoulder, while Theory yanked me into his arms.

"Call me when you're ready and I'll come get you."

"Are you really not going to let me drive?"

"Not right now, and Franks got somebody following Diamond so you guys should be good."

"She know that?"

Theory chuckled, "Nah, but it don't matter. She don't have a say in it right now."

"This is annoying," I said.

"Just be patient, it won't always be like this. I promise this will be over soon. Can you do that for me?"

"Yeah."

"Good, and don't think just 'cause you shut me down this morning that that's the end of it. I told you I have something for you." Theory kissed me before I could respond and then released me. "Go ahead inside so that I can leave," he said, with a smirk.

I just shook my head and left him standing their in-between his door and his car while he watched me walk inside the building. This man was always doing the most, but that was the thing I loved about him.

-6-

Theory

"Shouldn't you be laid up somewhere?" Josh asked, as soon as I climbed out of my car. He was waiting a few feet away and walked with me towards my office.

"I probably should be, but if I do that, then you guys don't get paid." We made our way through the shop area until we reached my office. I unlocked the door and Josh followed me inside, sitting down on the sofa across from my desk, while I sat down behind it.

"Yeah, you right. I got a few shorty's I need to chill with this weekend, so I need you to handle that." Josh looked at me with a grin, exposing his bottom row of platinum teeth. Josh was as hood as they came and looking at him you would swear he had been in an out of jail all his life, but actually he hadn't, not even once. He'd never sold drugs, never committed any thefts; in fact, his damn record was so clean that when I first hired him, I thought he was using a fake name.

That just goes to show, you never know who people really are, until you get to know them.

"What you need to do is stop wasting your money on these half-ass women you keep fucking around with, and find you somebody that's worth investing in," I said, after I logged into my computer.

"Nah, not yet. I'm young Theory; I'm just doing me right now, but it's coming, trust that."

"How old are you, Josh?" I looked up at him for a second.

"Shit, I'm just 24. I have time and plenty of it. I need to get this shit out my system before I find wifey. No sense in settling down when I know I'm not ready. That wouldn't be fair to either one of us." Josh rubbed his head and then smoothed his neatly trimmed beard.

I laughed. "I can respect that, at least your honest."

"Shit yeah, I don't want there to be any misunderstandings about it. I let these hoes know I'm just fuck and go right now. Anything extra, they can miss me with it," Josh chuckled to himself, about his affirmation. "And besides, I'm just trying to catch up with you, Theory."

"Then you need to be finding that one, 'cause I already have mine. Everything else was just temporary," I said, thinking about Rain. It was true. I moved around a lot, but only because I knew that there was only one person who deserved all of me, and until Rain came back, I was just buying time. Honestly, if I had never laid eyes on her again, I probably would have been by myself for the rest of my life. I just couldn't see being committed to anybody, but Rain, so if it wasn't her, it wasn't anybody.

"Word, when the fuck did that happen?" Josh sat up on the edge of the sofa and stared at me.

"It's always been that way; she just wasn't around, but she's back now."

"Damn, I need to meet whoever she is. She must be the truth if she got your ass on lock."

"Hell no, I'm not bringing her around your pimp, wannabe ass. You can forget that shit," I said, and laughed.

"Come on, Theory. You know that's not even me. I respect boundaries and I would never disrespect you like that, but I feel you though, keep wifey on lock."

"Don't you have some work to do?" Frank looked right at Josh when he entered my office. He walked over to him, Josh stood and they dapped each other.

"If my boss ain't complaining then your ass don't need to be complaining," Josh said.

"What the fuck ever. I'm still your boss, until I sign off on that shit and that hasn't happened yet." Frank sat down in front of my desk.

"Yeah aight, but I'm out. I need to go check on Sal. He's tripping over some order we just received. His OCD ass forever be stressed the fuck out." Josh shook his head and we all laughed, thinking about Sal. He was obsessed with detail, which made him good at his job, but annoying as hell.

"I'll get up with you later, Theory. Make sure that money hits the bank," Josh said, as he was leaving.

"You know I got you," I retuned just before he walked out, closing the door behind him.

"So, guess who our good friend, Niles, met up with last night?" Frank had a grin on his face like he was up to something.

I just stared at him, waiting.

"Sway." Frank said his name with a sort of satisfaction.

"Mac's dude?" I asked, already knowing the answer.

"Hell yeah. If that shit don't make you think bullshit, then I don't know what does."

I leaned back in my chair, processing for a minute. I knew good and damn well that Mac didn't send people after me like that. Shit, his ass was retired too, so there was nothing to gain from him taking me out, but Sway had a lot to gain. The only thing was that he would have to take out me, and Frank, in order for it to be beneficial to him.

"So, that means there's a hit on you, too," I said, randomly stating part of what I was thinking.

"Yeah, I was thinking that same shit. They would have to get rid of both of us in order to gain anything." Frank looked me, right in the eyes, before he continued. "What about Mac?"

"I don't know. I mean he's making money off Sway, so anything's possible, but it just wouldn't make sense for him to get involved in anything like that, not now. Mac's smart enough to know that we wouldn't just lay down about something like this, and Mac also knows that fucking with Niles is not worth the headache. Sway, on the other hand, is greedy. I can see the envy in his eyes every time he's around. He wants what we have and he's pissed that Mac's still controlling what he's doing. The question is, why the fuck would Niles trust that nigga?"

"Think about it, Thee. You'll have the detail shops, plus your cut of what we make on the streets. I have my cleaning services, but Niles doesn't have shit. He has all those damn kids and women, so why wouldn't he jump at the chance to keep all the profits. Think about how he kept stressing the fact that you were still going to make money off this shit, even after you got out. It's all making sense, now. I bet he was thinking he would use Sway to get rid of us, so that he could take over, but you know that shit wasn't happening. Even if he did take us down, Sway was probably thinking the same shit, and planning on getting rid of Niles. Niggas ain't got no loyalty, you already see that."

I couldn't help but laugh because the whole thing was so damn ridiculous, but it made perfect sense. Money made niggas stupid.

"Let's go," I stood, followed by Frank.

"Where we going?" Frank asked, looking at me confused.

"To tell Mac that he needs to find a replacement for Sway," I said, with a smirk.

Frank chuckled. "And if we don't like Mac's reaction?"

"You already know," I said, as we left the office.

It took us about twenty minutes to get to Mac's club. It was almost lunch and he basically lived there from the time it opened. *Bottom's Up* wasn't the biggest strip club in Atlanta, but it wasn't hurting for business in any way. This was the first one Mac opened after he got out the game, and he had recently opened his second one.

They knew us here so we got in with no issues, and found Mac sitting in front of the stage with a bottle full of Ace on the table, while he watched two of his girls, dance. Frank and I sat down at the table with him, and Mac waved his hand in the air, signaling for one of his hostess.

"I'm glad to see your ass is up and moving. I heard about what happened." Mac looked at me with sincerity, and I could tell that he actually meant what he said.

"'Preciate that. I'm still breathing, so I guess it wasn't my time," I said.

"To what do I owe the honor?" Mac asked, just as his hostess showed up.

"What can I get you guys?" she asked, smiling in my face a little too hard and invading my personal space.

"First, you can step your ass back and respect my personal space, and then you can get me an empty glass. Make sure that shit is clean, too."

Frank laughed before he looked out at her. She had a sour ass look on her face, but didn't say a word. "I'm good sweetheart," Frank said, with a smirk.

She turned and walked off with an attitude like it was supposed to affect my mood. That shit made me laugh.

"So, what's good with your boy, Sway?" Frank asked, now focused on Mac.

Mac chuckled, but kept his focus on the dancers for a few minutes longer, before he glanced at me and then looked at Frank.

"What you mean?" Mac asked.

The hostess returned and placed an empty glass down in front of me, but this time she kept her smile to herself, and made a point of staying out of my personal space. I lifted it to the light to inspect it, before I filled it with the Ace that Frank had on the table.

"You've known me since I was a kid, Mac. You put me on and I'm grateful for that, but that's as far as it goes. After all these years we've never had any problems, but we have one right now, and that's Sway. I don't know what type of loyalty you have to him, but that nigga is as good as dead as soon as I lay eyes on him. After that, we're good and we no longer have a problem anymore," I said.

Mac exhaled and focused on the stage again. He smiled at his dancers, clearly enjoying their performance, but he remained quiet for a few minutes. I finished my drink and waited. I could feel Frank's eyes on me. I knew that he was annoyed and ready to get this over with.

"You can't teach people the value of respect. I tried with Sway, but he's young and cocky. He thinks the world owes him something and he doesn't respect the value of working hard. He wants everything quick; I guess that's a generation thing." Mac finally turned to look at me.

"I don't really give a fuck about any of that. He has a bullet waiting on him which will either affect us, or it won't. That's your call, but I'm good either way and that nigga is dead either way," Frank said, after not housing the ability to hold his tongue any longer.

Mac glanced at Frank, but then focused on me. The relationship was with me; we had the most history. "You do whatever you have to do and I'm good with that. I told his ass that he would have to deal with the consequences of his actions, no matter what they were. Trust me when I say that I didn't have a hand in this, nor did I know about it, or I would have come to you. I respect you enough for that. You can either believe that, or don't, but it's the truth."

Mac extended a hand to me, which I shook, before I stood. He turned and offered the same to Frank, who hesitated, but then shook and with that, we were gone. Sway was 'bout to die and so was Niles. After that, hopefully I would be able to chill and focus my energy, on Rain.

*****

"What time are you going to be done today?" I asked, as soon as I hard Rain's voice. Frank dropped me off back at my shop and I had just finished up my payroll. I didn't really have shit else to do, so my mind kept drifting to Rain. I had to laugh at myself because no matter what was going on with my day, I always found myself thinking about her. She had totally changed the rhythm of my life from the second she showed up in Marty's.

"We have one more assignment and then I'm done, so probably a few hours and guess what?"

"What's that?"

"I got a raise and a contract, which means that they can't randomly fire me again, without being sued. I guess your little friend went above and beyond. You didn't sleep with her, did you?"

"Hell no. In fact, the last time I saw her I was about to slap the shit out of her dumb ass, and stop saying my friend. She ain't my anything and in fact, she ain't shit."

Rain laughed. "Why you so mad, you're the one who was dealing with her."

"Chill the fuck out with that shit and why are we even talking about her dumb ass?"

Again, Rain laughed because she knew I was pissed. "Where are you?"

"At my shop, but I'm heading out in a little while. We're going back to my house, so call me when you're done and I'll swing by and get you."

"Diamond can bring me," Rain said.

"Just do what I asked, please."

"Fine," she said, and then got quiet.

"You mad, Autumn Rain?"

"Nope."

"Tell me you love me then," I said with a smirk, knowing her stubborn ass was not feeling it.

"Bye, Thee."

I chuckled. "Your ass better not hang up this phone."

And of course, she did exactly what I knew she was going to do, and hung up. I just set my phone on my desk and smiled. I didn't really have shit else to do, so I decided to head across town to go check out Apple. We met a few years back at a club and kicked it for a minute, but then just ended up being friends. She was cool as hell and owned a tattoo shop, so anytime I needed work, I went to see her. Since I had time to kill, I decided to go get Rain's name redone somewhere else on my body, but I had no idea where, yet.

Apple's shop was a small location, but it was clean and always busy as hell. She had two other people who worked with her and they were always on point. I was just hoping that she would be able to fit me in, even though I knew she would move some things around to make it work. We were just cool like that.

"Damn stranger." Apple walked up to me the second I made my way through the door and threw her arms around me, which of course hurt like hell. She stepped back and looked at me, strangely.

"I'm a little sore right now," I said, and then offered up a smile.

"Come on, Thee, I know you didn't slip and let anybody lay hands on you," Apple said, with a smirk.

"Hell no, you know better than that, but they did catch my ass slipping and caught me with some heat."

"Who the hell is trying to take you out?" Apple looked at me concerned.

"Long story but, you busy right now?"

Again, her mocha face offered up a smile. "Never too busy for you, Theory, you know that. Come on." She turned to head towards the back and I watched as her ass, which was sitting lovely in a pair of painted-on black jeans, move down the hall. Apple was thick as hell and her name came from her apple-shaped ass. She told me the story of its origin once, while we were together.

I walked in her tattoo room and got comfortable, while she washed her hands and began getting her things ready.

"So, what you getting?" she asked, without looking at me, because she was setting up her station.

"I need a name, I just don't know where to put it, yet."

"A name?" Apple asked, with a smirk. She was now sitting beside me on her stool. "You giving up on your mystery girl?"

I laughed thinking about the fact Apple and I had several conversations about Rain. She was in love with the idea that I chose to love someone, who I might never see again.

"Actually no, it's her name that I'm getting. One of the bullets hit my left shoulder, so I need to get it somewhere else.

"Could you be any more perfect?" Apple teased, which made me burst out laughing.

"I am far from perfect, just ask Rain."

"Wait, so is she back?"

"How about right here?" I said, choosing to ignore her comment and pointing towards my neck. Apple and I were cool, but it seemed like the second a female caught wind that you were happy, it created feelings in them that they didn't know were there. I already had one fucked up situation with Lani, and I wasn't about to have another with Apple, so I kept my situation to myself.

I could tell she wanted to know more, but she left it alone and went to work.

"Well?" Apple asked, as she waited for me to respond. It was an hour later and she was done. I had Rain's name on the side of my neck to replace the one that was damaged on my shoulder.

"Shit, you already know. You always do work," I said, staring in the mirror.

"Thank you," Apple said, with a big grin. She was serious about her work and always put the time in, even with something as simple as a name. She took her time and made sure it was as perfect as it could be.

I paid, and then left the shop. I was about to head towards my house to hopefully catch a nap before Rain was ready for me to come get her. I didn't have any business being up and out all day, and my body was damn sure letting me know it.

-7-

Rain

"Oh my God, I just got my life," Diamond said dramatically, holding her chest and then laughed, which made me laugh.

"You keep that up and you're going to have to leave me here," I said, before I placed my camera into its bag.

Diamond looked at me confused.

"My damn head won't fit in the car if you keep pumping me up like that," I explained.

"Hell, forget that. You can get it and then some. You have no idea the nonsense I've had to deal with while you were gone. I did an article on Chance Taylor, you know dude who opened that clothing store downtown, and Hanson did the photos for me. Please tell me why I ended up with like two shots of the actual store, maybe one or two of Chance, and then the rest were of Chance's wife. Her ass wasn't even in the article. To say I was pissed was an understatement. I cussed his ass out in two languages."

I laughed at her because she was so serious. "Wait, I didn't know you spoke another language."

"Hell yeah! It's called 'nigga, no you didn't.'" Diamond tried her best to hold a straight face, but she couldn't and laughed.

"I'm not even messing with you." The more I thought about it, the more I laughed. She was too much for me.

"Girl, you know how it goes. You try to be civil and then that 'nigga, no you didn't' just takes over. A whole other language, just saying."

"Let's go, crazy. I want to take a look at these before Theory comes to pick me up."

"Girl, please, you know he's probably going to be there waiting on you because Larry is reporting to him every time your ass takes a breath."

"You need to stop," I playfully rolled my eyes at Diamond. "And would you stop calling that man Larry. That's just disrespectful."

"Shit, I need to call him something. He's been following me for almost a week and I don't know anything about him. So, to me he's Larry; Larry has a wife and two kids and can break bones with his bare hands." Diamond smiled at me just before she got in the driver's seat of her car. I placed my camera bag on the floor in the back seat and got in the passenger side.

"You are so damn stupid. Did you really just make up a whole life for that man?"

"I had to do something. It was creepy as hell having a stranger following me everywhere I go and then sitting outside my apartment, but I'm not stressed about

Larry. Larry is my dude. Creepy unnamed stalker guy, or Larry. So, as far as I'm concerned, his ass is Larry."

Diamond backed out of her parking spot, looking serious as hell. I just shook my head and laughed. It made sense, but it was still insane that she straight-up gave this guy a name and a life, but, that was Diamond for you.

Once we made it back to the office, Diamond went to go work on her article, while I went over my shots. I felt a rush just being in my office in front of my computer again. I couldn't help, but smile, but I was still fuming about the fact that any of this bullshit happened and it wasn't over for me. It wasn't going to be until I laid hands on her.

I spent some time going through my shots, and like always, got lost in what I was doing, so when Diamond showed up standing in my doorway asking me if Theory was still coming to get me, I immediately checked the time.

"Wow, I didn't know it was this late," I said, and lifted my phone off my desk to call Theory.

"Yeah, I just have to call him. You heading out?" I asked, as I unlocked my phone.

"Yes ma'am, about to head home, change, and then meet Frank for dinner." And of course she was smiling.

"Do I get to pick my dress?" I asked, mocking the way she was picking at me about Theory.

"Girl no, we're just chilling, but I like him though," Diamond said, blushing.

"Well, apparently he likes you, too. Thee seems to think he's stressing about Destiny." I looked at Diamond and waited. Hell, I was curious, too.

She rolled her eyes. "Trust me, Destiny is not the business and if Frank keeps putting it down then he don't have to worry about anybody."

"Well, I guess you said that, boo."

Diamond laughed. "Girl, bye, let me get out of here. I'll see you in the morning. Try not to get fired between now and then," she said, and then jetted out of my office before I could respond, because she knew she was dead ass wrong for that. I laughed to myself and then called Thee.

"What's up, Rain?" I could tell that Theory was sleep from how deep and heavy his voice sounded, which made me instantly want to be in his presence.

"So, I see you're finally acting right," I said, in reference to the fact that he was actually resting and not in the streets.

He let out a deep laugh. "Just getting ready for later."

"See, there you go, doing too much."

He laughed, again. "Give me a minute and I'll be on my way. Stay inside until I call you and tell you I'm outside."

"Yes, father," I said, sarcastically.

"Keep it up. You already got some shit coming," Theory said, and I could tell that he was moving around now.

"Bye, and hurry up," I said and ended the call, saved all my files, and got my stuff ready to go. I was missing my Theory and couldn't wait to be around him. It felt like things were starting to fall in place again. I just hope he could figure out his situation.

*****

"You know you didn't have to do this, right?" I looked up at Theory's neck as I lay across the sofa with my head in his lap, while he racked his finger through my hair. After he picked me up, we ran by his other house to get our stuff, so that we could go back to his main house. Theory ordered dinner and had it delivered, so we had eaten and were just chilling in the living room, talking.

"Is that too much commitment for you?" Theory looked down at me and smiled. Now, everywhere I go, everybody's gonna know who I belong to."

"All that means is they'll try harder. Commitment on a good man makes women lose their minds."

I looked up at Theory and could see him grinning. "What?" I asked, knowing he was thinking something crazy.

"So, I'm a good man?"

I laughed because I hadn't even realized what I said. "You're aight," I offered up a playful smirk.

"I'm more than aight, and you know it." Theory reached for my left hand and once he had it, his thumb glided across the tattoo on my wrist, before he spoke again.

"No matter what, it's always gonna be us. You know that right?"

I sat up and climbed into his lap, straddling his legs, before placing my hands on the sides of his face. I leaned in and kissed him. That was my answer, but the words were still necessary, so I replied with a simple, "Always."

A smile crept across his face as he stared into my eyes. We sat there with no words between us, just appreciating the fact that I had him, and he had me. The intensity of the moment that surrounded us was almost scary, because I could literally feel him in my soul. This man was my everything, and there was no doubt in my mind, that I was his.

"Is that a promise?" Theory's voice finally broke our moment and I couldn't help, but smile. I didn't want to talk anymore though, so I lifted my shirt over my head, before I stood and stepped out of the shorts that I was wearing. The rest of my clothes hit the floor right after, and then I found my spot again.

Once I was in place, Theory's hands slowly moved up my back, as his eyes traced my body. I was hungry for him, and my body was reacting like it was addicted to what I knew was to come.

I could feel his length beneath me, pressing against my ass, and it made my center throb. I needed to feel him inside me. While Theory's hands glided across my body, sending what felt like a wave of electrify through me, I lifted myself enough to release him. His eyes moved to our waist as he bit the corner of his lip, and stared at me for a brief moment, but the second I slid down on him and he filled me, his head went back, and his eyes closed.

"Damn Rain, that shit never gets old. I swear it's made just for me. This pussy is mine and I get pissed every time I think about the fact that you gave my shit away."

Theory's hands found my waist as I began gyrating my hips, slowly. This position was hard for me, because I could literally feel him tapping on my ribs every time he thrust in me. And right now he was holding me in place, so that I couldn't have any relief.

My mouth fell open, but no words escaped. That pushed him more as he leaned in and bit down on my shoulder, while increasing his pace. He had me wanting to scream out in pain, but I liked it, so I matched his rhythm, rotating my hips and bouncing against his pelvis, as he lifted me in the air, and then roughly forced my body back against his.

"Shit Rain, how the fuck you feel so good. You hold my shit so tight in there, I'd swear you had hands in that pussy, girl."

Theory was losing it because he fell back onto the sofa again, and his eyes were closed, while he tucked his bottom lip beneath his teeth. His grip tightened on my waist and I knew for sure I was going to have all types of bruises, but I didn't care, it was worth it. I loved the way he felt inside me, and the way he was handling me had every sensor in my body going off.

"Hold on, Thee, hold on," I panted out of breath. I felt my orgasm building, and my body was getting so sensitive that every time he touched me, I wanted to jump off his lap.

"Fuck that, cum for me Rain, let that shit go so I can stop holding mine." Theory's face turned serious as he leaned in and started sucking my nipples, rotating between each one. That was it, I couldn't take it anymore. My head fell back and a wave of heat rushed through my body, as I felt a warm flow between my legs. I fell onto Theory's chest and his arms locked behind my back, holding me in place against his rigid body, while he let out a loud grunt, and then slowly relaxed.

Neither of us spoke for a minute, just panting and heavy breathing, until Theory laughed.

"I might need to call Brooks. I think I just snapped some shit I wasn't supposed to." He held his head back and looked up at me. His face was covered in a layer of sweat and his hair curled slightly from the sweat that covered his head.

"You better not call him because he's going to ask you what you were doing," I frowned at Theory, who laughed again.

"You right, and I'm going to tell him you took advantage of me."

I snapped my head back again and narrowed my eyes at Theory. "I wish you would. I swear I'll kill you myself."

"No means no, Rain, and you're the one on top. I couldn't stop you because of my current injured state."

I balled up my fist and punched him in the chest before I hopped up. Again, his stupid ass laughed.

"I'm going to take a shower, but don't worry, you can tell him you won't have that problem anytime soon. So call him and I hope you enjoyed that because since you're so helpless, you've been officially cut off." I looked back at him over my shoulder as I collected my clothes.

Theory jumped up and grabbed me from behind. "No, hell, how about I just join you in the shower and take advantage of you, then we can call it even," he said, with a smirk as he turned me in his arms so that I was facing him.

"Yeah, I thought you might have a change of heart." I kissed him and we left the living room. My body might not have agreed to part two, but I missed my man, so it was happening.

*****

The room was dark and the house was quiet, as Theory and I lay silently in his bed. I felt at peace, like this right here was life and everything else about us was just details. It was almost impossible to describe, but I knew that no matter what, this was where I was supposed to be.

I closed my eyes and could feel myself drifting, and my mind took me back to the moment I knew that Theory would always be mine.

"Why you sitting there looking like that?" My eyes darted across the table of the booth I shared with Theory, and he was smiling, but I could see the concern in his eyes. He was always worried about me in one way or another.

I shrugged. "It's nothing," I replied, and took a sip of my vanilla.

"Don't let that bother you." I looked towards the counter and of course Theory's little crush was looking right at us. Her words constantly replaying in my head. You're his charity case boo, somebody like me is what he really wants.

Theory reached across the table and placed his hand on top of mine. "You know that's not true, right?"

I just looked at him and then out into the crowd at Marty's.

"Rain, I know you hear me. You know that's not true, right?" This time his voice flowed across the table with authority.

"What I know is that you're with me because you feel like you have to be." I hated that I felt that way, but I did; Theory was the perfect guy. It's not like he had anything to offer but himself, but that was enough. I knew that from the way females were constantly begging for his attention, and him occasionally entertaining their requests, meant he wanted them too, right? Why wouldn't he? We weren't together and he was a guy, but I secretly wanted that attention to be focused on me.

"You know me well enough to know that I don't do anything I don't want to do. I take care of you because I want to. If anything ever happened to you..."

He sat there for a second like he was trying to find the words and then he continued. "If you tell me that I'm what you want then no one else will ever matter.

Ever. I promise you that. All you have to do is tell me Rain. I'll choose you every time, but you have to tell me that's what you want."

That was the day before we spent out last night together. The next morning, I was being escorted out of the hotel room we shared, while Theory watched helplessly. I could see the pain in his eyes, because he felt like he failed me—that he failed us—but I knew better. I didn't blame him and I never would, but I knew right then that he would always be mine.

.

-8-

Theory

I could hear Rain moving around the room and then entering the bathroom. If she called herself trying to be quiet, she was failing miserably. For the first time in the past few days, I woke up without feeling pain in every inch of my body. I knew I still had a long way to go, but at least I knew I was getting better.

After I sat up and grabbed my phone, I called Frank to see if we had any new information. I was getting just as impatient as he was, which led to my decision that Niles and Sway would be handled tonight. I wasn't really worried about myself, but anything that put Rain in danger was a problem for me, and I had to make sure it was taken care of.

"Yo, what's good Frank?"

"Shit, chillin. I'm about to head home in a few and then run by my dealership. We ready to make some moves?"

"Wait, it's seven in the morning, where the fuck you at?"

Frank laughed. "I'm with Diamond. Your ass just kidnapped Rain, so I'm not really feeling her being alone right now."

I chuckled. "Yeah, whatever muthafucker. I'm sure it's all about safety."

"Fuck you, Thee. I told you I'm just chillin', nothing more, nothing less. But anyway, what's the plan? I'm ready to handle some things. The more I think about his snake ass, the more pissed I get."

Before I could answer, I looked up and Rain was coming out the bathroom. She walked over and sat on the bed next to me, and started inspecting my body. She was playing doctor, but my body was thinking something totally different.

"Yeah, we can do that. I'm about to get up now so that I can take Rain to work. I'll meet you at your spot, but I have to run by and see Alex first."

Rain immediately stopped what she was doing when I mentioned Alex's name, and I laughed because she looked like she wanted to slap me for just mentioning it.

"Aight, that works. Just call me when you're heading this way."

"Aight, bet." I ended the call and dropped the phone on the bed, before I pulled Rain against my body.

"Why are you going to see her?" Rain asked, trying to pull away from me, but I held her in place.

"She's still my lawyer Rain, but you already know you don't have to stress that," I said, and leaned down to kiss her, but she yanked her head back.

"Trust me, I'm not worried about her, but that don't mean I want you all up in her face. In fact, I'm going with you and then you can drop me off at work."

I shook my head and laughed. "You don't trust me?"

"I trust you, but I want to slap the shit out of that hoe, and today just might be that day," Rain said, and I knew she was serious.

"Hell no, I'm not taking you up there so that you can put your hands on that girl. That shit ain't happening. I told you she's still my lawyer and until I find a new one, I need her to cooperate." I stole a quick kiss and then released my hold on Rain so that I could get out of the bed. She took my place, but was sitting on the edge peering at me like she wanted to jump on me.

"I won't touch her, but I'm going and you shouldn't have a problem with that. How is she even your lawyer? You sure you weren't fucking her?"

"Rain, chill with that shit. I was fucking a lot of females, I admit that, but she damn sure wasn't one of them. I don't swap pussy and she used to fuck with Niles."

I could tell I struck a nerve with her by admitting my past, but she knew me so there was no need to sugarcoat it. And besides, it was temporary; if she was here, I wouldn't have fucked with any of them and she knew it, so she didn't have a damn thing to worry about.

"Well, I'm still going," she said, looking me right in my eyes with a hard stare.

I just shook my head, left her sitting there, and walked into the bathroom. After I finished my shower, the room was empty, so I got dressed figuring Rain was likely in the kitchen. Once I was done, I followed the smell of coffee and found Rain leaning against the island with a mug in her hands.

I kissed her on the cheek before I opened the refrigerator to get some orange juice, moved to the cabinet to get a glass, and then filled it.

"Can we do something later?" Rain asked, setting her mug on the top of the island before she leaned across it, resting on her elbows.

"Something like what?" I asked, after I downed half of my juice.

"I don't know… maybe dinner or something and with Diamond and Frank."

I thought about the fact that Frank and I planned on killing Niles and Sway at some point today, and I couldn't really map that out.

"We'll see. I've got some things to take care of with Frank, but if we can get it handled then yeah, we can do that."

Rain looked at me strange for a minute. She knew what I did, but we still hadn't had a real in-depth conversation about what that really meant.

"Will you try please? I miss just hanging out and I wanna do that with you guys," Rain said, looking partially disappointed at the idea that it might not happen. She knew how to get to a brother with those damn sad eyes.

"I promise; I'll do what I can, but we need to talk later. I have a few things I need to discuss with you."

"About Niles and what happened?"

I finished my juice, set my glass in the sink, and then kissed her. "Just things; come on, let's go."

"You need to eat something Thee," Rain said behind my back as I left the kitchen.

"I'll grab something out, I'm good right now."

Roughly forty-five minutes later, Rain and I were walking through the lobby of the building that Alex worked in, hand in hand. When we stepped off the elevator, I could see her expression drop and she was looking like she was ready for war. I had to laugh to myself because she was mad as hell for no reason, but that shit was cute a fuck.

When we reached the receptionist, she looked up at us strangely, but her eyes stayed on Rain, while she spoke to me. I knew it was because her bitch ass ex worked here too, and she recognized Rain, probably from visiting him. Now I was pissed.

"She's in her office waiting, Mr. Bryant. I'll take—"

"Nah, you're good ma, I know where it is," I said, grabbing Rain's hand again and pulling her body close to mine. Knowing that her ex worked here had me in defense mode, even though I knew he didn't have shit on me. It was just the principle.

We walked through the office and I could feel a few eyes on us. Mostly women, who I knew were sweating me and when we walked into Alex's office, her damn mouth fell open and all the color drained from her face.

"The fuck you looking all crazy for?" I wasn't in the mood to deal with her bullshit, and I needed this to go smooth, so that Rain didn't jump on her ass.

Alex's eyes fell on Rain and I felt Rain try to yank her hand away from mine, but I held it tighter so that she couldn't.

"Umm, so I did like you asked and got all of your files together." Alex sat down and started fumbling with some folders on her desk, but she kept looking up and stealing glances at Rain. She clearly was not happy about the fact that I brought her, but that shit was kind of funny though.

"Bitch, keep your eyes off me and do what he's paying you to do. If you like what you're looking at that damn bad, shoot me your number and I will shoot you a selfie," Rain said, narrowing her eyes at Alex. I chuckled.

"Rain, chill and shit down." Rain looked up at me like I had two heads and didn't move, until I sat down in one of the chairs in front of Alex's desk, and pulled her into my lap. Once I had my arms around her waist and my chin resting on her shoulder, she relaxed a little, and Alex got even more pissed.

"Look ma, you pulled some foul shit and I can't fuck with you like that. So, for now I just needed to make sure everything is in order, until I can find a new lawyer. But trust me, if you try some fuck shit then it won't go well for you. All I need you to do right now is make sure Niles's name is off anything that belongs to me. I'll be back later to pick up the paperwork and once I get Frank to sign off, I'll bring that shit back to you to file legally for me. Until then, I don't need shit from you and I don't want you fucking with me."

Again Alex was at a loss for words. She couldn't keep her damn eyes off Rain, so I called her name to get her attention. "Alex, did you hear what the fuck I just said?"

She nodded, "Yeah, we're good." Her face was all screwed up, but she wasn't about to say shit because she knew better.

"Aight then, I'll be back in a few hours. Make sure you have that shit ready." I pointed to her desk and then lifted Rain so that I could stand.

"Fine," was all Alex said and I laughed before heading towards her door, but Rain's hostile ass couldn't let it go. She stepped towards Alex's desk and slapped the shit out of her so quickly, that neither of us saw it coming.

Alex jumped up and grabbed her face. "Really, Theory, are you going to let her put her hands on me?"

I shrugged, "Shit, that's on you. You ain't my girl, so call your nigga if you need somebody to defend you."

Rain laughed and pointed her finger in Alex's face. "Stay in your lane or trust me, that's not even close to the damage that you can expect."

Then, just like that, she pushed past me and stormed out of Alex's office. I laughed and followed her little angry ass, and caught her arm once we were in the hallway in front of the elevator.

"Why you put your hands on her like that? I told you I wasn't fucking with her," I smiled at Rain.

"I just don't like her," she snapped.

"That better not be about that nigga," I said, pointing back towards their offices.

Rain's head whipped around so fast that she probably pulled something. "Hell no, it's not about him!

It's about the fact that she disrespected me about you at Frank's, and I just don't like her snake ass."

I grabbed Rain by the waist and kissed her to calm her down, but the second I let her go, her bitch ass ex came walking out the office, with Alex behind him. Here we fucking go. As much as I wanted to fuck him up, I was trying to be civil, but if he stepped to me on some bullshit, that was a wrap.

"Really, Rain? So I guess you with this nigga now and you're back to your old ways. I should have known better than to think you could be something more than a street kid, I don't know what I was thinking."

Next thing I know, I felt bones cracking under my fist as they made contact with his face. I tried my best to kill that nigga and got pretty damn close, until Rain stopped me. She grabbed my arm and pulled me back.

"Theory stop, he's not even worth the energy. Let's go before they call the cops."

I stood and looked down as Alex tried to help him up, but he shoved her back and Rain took a step towards him.

"What you were thinking is that you wanted more from me than I was ever going to give, so you went and found this bottom-shelf bitch. You can call me whatever you want, but bottom line is this… we both know that if I would take you back even now, your ass would be all smiles."

Rain pointed at Alex. "That bitch will never be me and you damn sure will never be Theory, not even close. Have a good life, both of you."

Rain marched her little ass to the elevator, dragging me with her, and punched the button with so much force that I knew her damn finger had to hurt. After fucking him up, I wasn't even mad anymore. That was a long time coming, but my damn body did not agree with what I had just done, because I could feel it all over.

When the doors opened, Rain stepped inside. I followed while Alex and her man were in a heated argument. I thought that shit was funny as hell. Alex wanted me, he wanted Rain, but they called themselves being together. What the fuck?

Rain still hadn't said a word to me and when we got off on the first floor, she stepped out and I grabbed her arm.

"You can be mad at them all you want, but you better calm that shit down because they're not here and I am." I looked down at Rain who had her arms crossed, looking like she would smack me at any second.

It took her a minute, but she finally relaxed and smiled. "I'm not mad at you; hell, I'm not even mad at their dumb asses. That was kind of funny, wasn't it?"

"Hell no, that shit wasn't funny, got me up there showing my ass."

"Shut up, yes it was and you know it, but thank you." She slid her arms around my waist and then looked up at me.

"The fuck you thanking me for. I beat that nigga's ass because he had it coming," I said, with a smirk.

"Doesn't matter. Either way I know you always got me."

I leaned down and pecked her on the lips. "Hell, you knew that already, now let's go before they fire your ass again for being late."

I tried to move back, but Rain nailed me in the arm with her little ass fist. "Aight, chill with that because I'm not gonna hit you back, but I will make you pay." I reached for her hand and led the way out the building.

"Whatever, you know better."

I just smiled. Her and that smart ass mouth was too much, but that was my, Autumn Rain. Wouldn't change a damn thing about her, good or bad.

9

Rain

"So, that's how we're doing it? You get your little contract and you just run out and show up when you want to." Diamond sat on the edge of my desk, grinning at me.

"See, there you go," I said and laughed.

"I'm just saying boo, you were supposed to be here an hour ago." Diamond looked down at her watch and then back at me.

"Whatever, I had to go with Theory to see his lawyer."

"Oh Lord, get your stuff so we can go. You can tell me all about it on the way to meet Jax."

"Who's Jax?" I asked, lifting my camera bag off the floor and then following Diamond out of my office.

"You'll see when we get there. He's a new artist on Loyalty and this nigga is… oh Lord, I don't even have words."

Diamond fanned herself dramatically, which made me laugh. "Um, do I need to tell we need a new assignment. I don't think Frank would appreciate you lusting over whoever this Jax is."

"Girl please, my damn eyes work and so do his. I don't want that nigga, but it don't mean he's not worth looking at. Frank don't need to know a damn thing," Diamond said, rolling her eyes.

"But you worried about it though," I said from behind her.

"Shut up Rain, ain't no body worried about Frank," Diamond said over her shoulder, but I could see the smile. Yeah, she was feeling him. That was cool though. I like Frank.

Once we were in Diamond's car headed across town, I began filling her in on what went down with me, Alex, Jamel, and Theory. She couldn't stop laughing at the whole thing.

"So, you just hauled off and smacked the shit out of her? Damn, I hate I missed that. I knew your ass could get it in."

"I didn't fight the hoe, I just smacked her."

"But she didn't try to hit your ass back, so you must have smacked some sense into her ass. She knew better. And then her dumb ass had the nerve to ask Theory to defend her. What the fuck? I gave that hoe too much credit."

"You're stupid, but you're right though. My damn hand was sore as hell after that. Shit, it still hurts now." I held it up and started examining it.

"And then Theory beat Mel's ass. Damn Rain, you should have called me," Diamond said, looking at me serious as hell.

"How the hell was I supposed to do that?"

"You could have been like, hold on Thee, don't hit that nigga until Diamond gets here. I know she would love to see this."

I couldn't control my laugh. "You are insane."

Diamond laughed with me. The rest of the ride, we joked about what happened and she filled me in on how Destiny had recently started stalking her, blowing up her phone, and acting crazy. She was thinking about getting a restraining order, but was trying to give it time to see if things died down. When we reached *Loyalty Records,* we grabbed our stuff, got out, and made our way up to their suite. The receptionist pointed towards the recording studio where we were supposed to meet Jax, and when we got to the door, Diamond knocked and walked in.

I had to do a double take because dude was all that. He was sitting in front of the sound board leaning back, on his cell phone, but the second we were in the room, he looked up and smiled. Damn, his ass was almost pretty he looked so damn good. He had flawless mocha skin and hazel eyes, his hair was cut low with waves for days, and his face housed a low-trimmed beard, which he reached up and rubbed the second he laid eyes on us. He was dressed casually in a pair of sweat pants and matching sweat shirt, and a spotless pair of Air Max.

"Yo' man, let me hit you back. Some beautiful young ladies just walked in."

Oh shit, let me get my stuff together. Good Lord, this man was fine.

He ended his call, stood, and after he folded his arms across his chest, he looked down at us and smiled.

"You must be Rain and Diamond?"

"Yes, pleased to meet you," I responded. Okay, I was out of my trance and ready to work.

"Which one are you?" he asked, as he towered over me, grinning.

"Rain, and this is Diamond."

Diamond finally got her head right too, and spoke up. "I'm assuming you're Jax," she said.

"The one and only," he winked at Diamond.

"So, are we working in here?" I asked, stepping around Diamond, shoving her with my body just a little.

"I'm cool with that, if that works for you."

Detroit wants me to do some studio shots to put out for promo. I'm not with that shit, but I guess he pays the bills."

The second he said that name, I got pissed. I started looking around the studio and sure enough, I saw pictures of Lani on the wall with various artists, and one with her and an older dude, who I assumed was her father.

"Is that that him, Detroit?"

"Yeah, what's up, you know him?"

"Nah, not really."

Diamond looked at me funny and then turned her focus back to Jax, "Okay, so let's get started. I'm going to use my recorder, if that's okay with you."

"Whatever you need lil' mama. This is your shit." He smiled and sat back down in his chair. "You got me however you want me."

I looked at Diamond and shook my head. Please let this man be respectful. I didn't need anybody else on Theory's hit list.

We all got comfortable and went to work. I began taking random shots, while Diamond did her interview. I listened and stayed out of the way, but Jax seemed like a pretty decent guy. He offered up a little flirting every now and then, but nothing over the top. He actually turned out to be nothing like I expected. Most men who looked like him knew it, which generally led to them acting like they owned the rights to every woman within eyesight, but I didn't get that feeling from him. Jax came up in the streets, but his first love was singing, so that's what got him here. He let us listen to a few songs and they were actually pretty decent. Kind of R&B with a street edge to them.

Things went smooth and when we were done, Diamond and I packed up and said our goodbyes. Jax invited us to his album release party, which I knew I wasn't going to, since Lani would likely be there. Just as we were about to leave, some loud mouth girl came busting through the door with an equally loud chick behind her. They were so wrapped up in their conversation that they didn't realize we were in the studio, but the second I laid eyes on them, I was instantly annoyed.

"Rain, what the fuck you doing in here with my man?" Charlotte asked, quickly moving to Jax and wrapping her body around his.

He leaned down and kissed her on the cheek. "They just did an interview and photo shoot for *Urban Pride*. I told you that's what I was doing today," he explained.

"You know her?" Diamond asked.

"Yeah, she's my sister," I said, with very little emotion.

"So, this is the sister you're always talking about? Damn, small world, huh?" Jax said and Charlotte looked at him annoyed. I laughed at her jealous ass.

"Yeah, but they ain't close," her little loud mouth friend said as she moved closer to Jax and Charlotte.

Jax looked at me and then Charlotte, confused. "You always act like you miss her when you talk about her." Again, Charlotte looked like she wanted to scream at him to shut up.

"She's my sister, of course, I miss her." Charlotte walked over to me invading my personal space, and throwing her arms around me. I rolled my eyes, hugged her back and then quickly moved away from her.

"I have your information. I'll send you the proofs for your approval before we print them," I said, as I lifted my camera bag.

"'Preciate that, but I'm not worried. Seemed like you knew what you were doing. I'll walk you guys out though."

I laughed because Charlotte looked pissed that he offered.

"Nah, we're good, but thanks," Diamond said, knowing that I was going to object.

"Aight, take it easy," Jax said, as he sat down and Charlotte found her way onto his lap. It was just like her to latch herself onto a guy, like Jax. I actually felt sorry for him.

"So, the infamous loner has a sister." Diamond wore a smirk as we made our way out the building towards her car. For her, Charlotte was a missing piece to my puzzle, but to me, she was just trouble.

"Yeah, and you can see how much that means to me. Let's just say we're not close."

Diamond laughed, "I can see that. Now I know why you don't like people; I don't like her and I don't even know her."

"I like people, I just don't want them all up in my business."

"Whatever, let's go eat so that you can tell me all about that accident waiting to happen."

"Lord, that would take a lifetime." I shook my head thinking about all the issues I had with my sister, as Diamond and I got in her car to leave.

*****

"So this is your spot, huh?" Diamond looked around Marty's, and smiled.

"Yeah, I guess you can say that. We used to come here all the time so it kind of is."

"It's cute in here just like you two. Y'all are so damn cute," Diamond said, with a smirk and then lifted her menu.

"Forget you, hoe. Don't hate," I laughed.

"I'm not, I'm just saying, y'all got some hood fairytale shit going on and its cute. I'm jealous, boo. I want that forever kind of love, too."

"Then pick a lane and stay with Frank. I can see that for you."

"Girl please, Frank damn sure ain't no fairytale. He's not Theory. I mean he's cool and everything, so we'll see."

"Girl bye, you need to stop playing. You know you want that man."

"Jury's still out on that one. So, what's the deal with your sister? You two are nothing alike."

I laughed. "Dang, how you say that and you only met her for all of five seconds?"

"I know people and I knew her the second I laid eyes on her. She's selfish, spoiled and ratchet as hell. What is she a stripper, video girl, or both?"

I couldn't control my smile. "Stripper."

"See, I told you I knew her."

"Trust me, everything you're thinking is probably true. How on earth she is with a guy like Jax, is insane to me, but then again, Charlotte could always get them, she just couldn't keep them."

"She's pretty, so I'm sure that has a lot to do with it, but damn, his ass is too fine for her nonsense."

"You need to calm all that down, over there having mini orgasms and shit," I laughed and pointed at Diamond.

"Shut up hoe, you know you were drooling. Your damn eyes work just like mine." Diamond snapped.

"Hell yeah, you can't help, but to. He's worth drooling over, but he's too pretty for me. I can't be fighting with my man over mirror time. Men like that require too much attention."

"You so damn crazy, but you right though. The only thing I can do with a man like that is look at him, but I bet he can lay it down though. He just looks like he got some shit with him."

I laughed. "You need to stop. I'm not even going there with you like that, but you're right, though."

Diamond looked past me and frowned, so I turned to see what she was looking at, and our babysitter "Larry" was standing outside Marty's on the phone, which I thought was weird because he never got out the car, he just followed up.

"I hope he don't come in here trying to sit with us," Diamond said and rolled her eyes, but a seconds later, Theory and Frank walked up, and they all dapped each other. Larry pointed inside and then walked off, while Frank and Theory walked in and made their way over to us.

"So, that's how we're doing it?" Diamond rolled her eyes at Frank, as he slid into the booth next to her.

"What?" he asked, after he kissed her on the cheek.

"You already got Larry following us and now you got him telling you where we are. Damn, I feel so violated."

"Who the fuck is Larry?" Theory asked, looking at Diamond, and then me.

We both looked at each other and laughed. "Ah, damn Diamond, I told you I shouldn't have hugged that dude. I knew it was strange that he didn't know who gave him instructions to follow us," I said, just to mess with Theory and it worked, because his jaw tightened and he was about to get up to go find whoever this Larry person was.

"You better stop playing with him like that before he mess around and hurt some innocent person, thinking it's Larry," Diamond said, pointing her finger at me.

"Somebody better tell me who the fuck Larry is," Theory said, looking right at me.

"Larry is the guy Frank had following Diamond. She said it was creepy to have some unnamed stalker person following her, so she named him Larry, and made up a whole story about him."

I could see Theory relax a little, but I could tell he was annoyed. "Keep playing. She's right, you're gonna fuck around and make somebody lose their life," Theory said, as he leaned back and placed his arm across the back of the booth.

"Awe, were you jealous?" I moved my body close to his and he tried to act like he didn't want me near him, until my hand moved across his leg, but he grabbed my wrist to stop me.

"Hell yeah, I was jealous. I better be the only nigga you put your arms around and I put that on everything." Theory leaned towards me and pecked me on the lips.

"Why are you here, anyway?" Diamond asked, looking at Frank

"You not happy to see me?" he asked, before he grabbed her chin and then kissed her.

"I'm always glad to see you, but that don't explain why you're randomly popping up on us," Diamond said.

"You got a problem with that?" Frank had a cocky grin on his face.

"Maybe, I do."

"Maybe, I don't give a fuck," Frank said, before he picked up the menu's that Diamond had been looking at, and she just rolled her eyes.

"Did you order already?" Theory asked, when he saw the waitress heading our way.

"Nope, did you eat something this morning?"

"Yeah, but I can still eat."

"Are you guys ready to order?"

I looked up when I heard the attitude in her question. *Here we go with this shit again*, I thought, but it seemed like her attitude came more from the fact that she hated her job versus her being interested in Theory, which I was grateful for. But hey, I had already slapped one bitch today, what was one more?

"Let me get two slices and a Dr. Pepper, and she'll take a large vanilla milkshake and a large fry." Theory looked at me to be sure I didn't want to add anything, but I nodded and he turned his attention back to the waitress.

"You know what you want?" Frank asked, looking at Diamond.

"Burger and fries with a large Pepsi," Diamond said.

"Let me get the same," Frank said, and then she turned and walked off.

"See, y'all so cute; he even orders for you," Diamond said, grinning at me and Theory.

"You need to stop, like seriously."

Theory just chuckled. "I have a few things to handle with Frank, so I need you to head to my house and stay there until I get there." He looked at Diamond. "In fact, if you don't mind taking her then y'all can just chill until we get back. You good with that Frank?"

"Yeah, that's straight, you good with that?" he looked down at Diamond to get her approval.

"She's good with that," I answered for her.

"Hello, I can speak for myself," Diamond said, playfully rolling her eyes. "Yeah, I guess that's cool, as long as you let Larry chill with us."

"You think that shit is funny now, just wait until later," Frank said, mugging Diamond which made her laugh.

"Whatever."

I stuck my tongue out at Diamond and she shot me a bird. After our food came, we all ate and chilled for a while, until Theory and Frank said they had to leave. They were real vague about what they had to do later, but I had a feeling that it involved Niles. Honestly, I didn't really care as long as Theory was good. I couldn't take any more stress right now, especially since it seemed like things were finally starting to level out.

10

Theory

"You ready for this shit?" Frank looked over at me displaying a grin. You would think it was Christmas or something the way his ass kept grinning. If I messed around and called this shit off right now, I had a feeling Frank would probably shoot me.

I released a muffled laugh and looked around. Frank and I waited until the night fell to ride up on Niles, so that we wouldn't be seen.

"Hell yeah, when am I ever not ready?" I reached under my seat and wrapped my hand around my .9. Once I had eyes on it, I chambered the first round. People who say that revenge doesn't solve anything, must have never really actively participated in it. True enough it didn't change the situation, but it damn sure made you feel good. I had a sense of peace settling in already, just knowing that I had a bullet with Niles and Sway's name on it.

"Aight then, let's get this over with. I've got some act-right to dish out after this." Frank had a smirk on his face and I knew he was thinking about Diamond. Yeah, she had his ass. I just hoped it worked out for him.

We climbed out of the black Infinity that we used for situations like this, but before I shut the door, I picked up the stack of papers that Alex gave me for Niles to sign, and affixed them under my shirt. After that, Frank and I walked up to Niles' front door.

"You really 'bout to make that nigga sign off on that shit before you put a bullet in him? Damn, Thee, that's some foul shit," Frank laughed.

"Hell, yeah. If I don't do it now, then there's a bunch of other legal shit to do and I don't want that nigga's name on my shit."

Frank just shook his head and laughed. We had people on Niles all day, so we knew that he was currently home and entertaining. My main concern was making sure his kids weren't there with him. They were about to be fatherless, but I wasn't so heartless that I would make that happen while they were there. That just wasn't me.

Once we were on Niles' front porch, Frank dug in the flower pot and found the key that Niles left for his female visitors. Our guys had been watching him all week and discovered it. Niles was too cheap to pay for a security system and just elected to post the signs in his yard and on the window, but Frank and I knew for a fact that he didn't actually have anything set up.

"This nigga is dumb as fuck. First, you leave a key and then you don't even have security. He must really think he got away with this shit, because he just chillin' all unprotected," I whispered to Frank, once we were inside. The house was dark, but we had been there several times before, so we were familiar with it.

Frank laughed. "Well, he's in for a big ass surprise."

We started up the stairs and the closer we got to the top floor, we could hear two voices. One was clearly Niles, while the other was a female's that I swore sounded like Savannah, but she stopped talking, so I didn't have enough time to figure it out.

As soon as we were outside Niles' bedroom door, Frank posted up on one side while I placed my hand on the actual door to push it open. It was already cracked, so I peeked inside and chuckled when I saw a female on her knees in front of Niles. This bitch, I swear.

"Well, well, I guess you found that dick to suck after all," I said, with a grin when I stepped in the room. Savannah's head whipped around while Niles went to fumbling, reaching for the gun he had next to him on the bed.

"Hands up muthafucker, you know it's not going down like that," Frank said, with his gun pointed at Niles' head.

"Get your ass up and you," I pointed at Niles, "pull your fucking pants up."

Niles looked from me to Frank before he reached down and grabbed his pants, which were around his ankles, and pulled them up around his waist. Savannah also reached for her clothes seeing as how she was naked, but Frank spoke up.

"Ain't nobody say shit about you putting on no damn clothes. Drop that shit and sit down next to his dumb ass."

"I'm not having sex with you, so you can just shoot me if that's what you're thinking," she said, like she had a say in anything that was about to go down.

"Bitch, don't nobody want that rundown shit you got between your legs, trust me, I already made that mistake once, and I will not be doing it again."

"Damn, you hit that shit Thee, you ain't shit nigga. You knew I wanted to fuck her," Franks said, and laughed.

"Trust me, I saved you on that one, bruh."

"Fuck you Theory," she yelled, shooting me a bird. I could see Niles out the corner of my eye reaching for his gun again, so I fired a shot right next to his hand. He snatched it back and looked up at me, while Savannah screamed.

"The fuck Theory, you almost shot me," Niles said, looking at me like I was crazy.

"Shit nigga, you did shoot me. Almost and did, I think I win, don't you?" I said, looking right at Niles.

"Is that what this is about? I know you don't think I had anything to do with that Theory. Come on, we're boys. Me, you, and Frank. Come on, Frank, I know you don't believe that, do you?" Niles looked nervous as hell as he rambled on. Savannah moved away from him, scooting to the corner of the bed that was farthest way from Niles.

I laughed, sarcastically. "Hell no, I don't think you had anything to do with it. I mean, we're boys, right Niles? Because if you did, that would be the dumbest decision you ever made in your life. Dumbest, life threatening, decision that you ever made in your life, and I know that there is no way that you would ever be that stupid. Right Frank, he wouldn't be that stupid would he?"

"Nah, Thee, I just can't believe that he would be that damn stupid," Frank said, with a grin.

"But, I mean he is fucking this bitch and that's pretty stupid. I don't even see any condoms around, so that means he was gonna go up in that shit raw. That does say a lot about his decision-making skills."

"You know what, fuck you and you," Savannah said, standing again to reach for her clothes. "I don't know what little pissing match you have going on here, but it doesn't involve me, so I'm leaving."

"Bitch, sit yo' ass down." Frank pointed his gun right at her head. "Did anybody ask you to speak or move? Keep that shit up and you won't ever make it out of here."

"You can't kill me. The cops will—"

Frank fired a bullet that flew right past her head causing her to duck, placing a hand over each ear.

"Shut the fuck up and sit yo' ass down. The cops ain't gone do shit and if you're lucky enough to make it out of here alive, I wish your dumb ass would go to the damn cops, talking some nonsense. I'll kill your whole damn family and won't even give it a second thought," Frank said.

This time Savannah decided to take him serious. She sat down on the bed again and didn't say another word.

"Good girl. It's a shame your fine ass is nasty as hell or I would fuck you just to shut your annoying ass up. But I wouldn't do my girl like that, 'cause ain't no telling what that shit is infested with." Frank grabbed himself and smiled at Savannah. I just shook my head; this fool was already on one-hundred and still rising.

"Now, back to your dumb ass. I just had a few questions, but I need you to sign this shit first." I pulled out the papers that Alex prepared, for me to get Niles name off all my shit. I wasn't about to let his family get a dime from me after he died, and his ass was dying tonight.

Niles looked at me like he was about to throw up. He was sweating and I could see the fear in his eyes. He knew he fucked up and was about to pay for it.

"Anything. Anything you want to know Theory, just ask me, but I promise you I didn't have anything to do with you getting shot."

I chuckled. "Yeah, well I'll be the judge of that." I tossed the papers to him and looked around for a pen, which I found on the dresser. I tossed that to him as well, and he began mindlessly scanning the documents.

"Just fucking sign where the green labels are. You don't need to read shit." I was already annoyed and he damn sure wasn't helping. I was strongly considering just shooting his ass as soon as he was done. This nigga wants to try and read shit when he knew that he was about to die. Niles started scribbling his signature throughout the documents, likely because he was scared as shit and praying that it increased his odds at living. He was going to roll with it because he didn't want to die. In his mind, if signing over the business to me meant that he would be breathing tomorrow, then he would do it.

"See, there you go trying to run shit. If you're the damn judge, then let me be the fucking lawyer. I'll ask the questions," Frank said, looking right at me.

Niles' stare went back and forth between me and Frank before he focused on Frank. I grabbed the papers he had just finished signing and placed them under my shirt again.

"So, how many shooters were there?" Frank moved close to Niles and folded his arms across his chest, while I stood back and kept my gun pointed at Niles' head.

"What do you mean how many shooters? How would I know that?" Niles asked, looking between Frank and I again.

"Well, I seem to remember you asking Rain if she saw the two shooters' faces?" Frank asked, but before Niles could open his mouth to respond, I rocked the shit out of him. I hit him so hard blood instantly flew out of his mouth and splattered on his bed.

"The fuck, Thee. You can't just hit that nigga. Let him answer first," Frank laughed.

"That was for fucking with Rain. I know your ass knew better than that." I pointed at Niles as he sat up and grabbed his jaw. "Now answer the fucking question."

"I don't know; how the fuck would I know? I told you I didn't have anything to do with this. I don't know why you don't believe me." Niles was damn near begging for mercy and I was over it. I lifted my gun and shot him in the head.

Savannah screamed, hit the floor, and cowered into a fetal position, crying.

"Damn bitch, will you shut the fuck up. You wanted to hang with hood niggas, well this is what the fuck you get when you hang with hood niggas. So stop all that damn crying before I shoot your ass too," I said, causing Savannah to cover her mouth to muffle her cries. She looked up at me with fear in her eyes.

"What the fuck was that. No warning or anything?" Frank said, now looking at me as he reached beside Frank's body and picked up his gun.

"Didn't your ass say that I could be the judge? Shit, I found his ass guilty and death was his punishment," I said, with a smirk.

Frank just laughed. "What about her?"

We both looked at Savannah and she looked up at us like a lost child.

"You wanna go home?" I asked.

She looked at me and then at Frank, before nodding.

"Get dressed," I said, and she hesitated for a minute, but eventually grabbed her clothes and started covering her body.

"I'll call to get this shit cleaned up," Frank said.

He left the room with his phone to his ear while I pointed at the bed. "Sit down."

Savannah was dressed, but she looked down at the bed where Niles' body was, and shook her head to tell me no.

"Sit your ass down, that wasn't a question."

She sat of the very edge of the bed as far away from Niles as she could get.

"You get to leave, but trust me, if you think about doing anything stupid, I will come looking for you and the cops can't protect you. If you think you can tell them about what happened here, they'll think you're crazy. The house will be spotless and there won't be a body, so take your ass home and go about your happy little, fucked up life as usual, and you live. Understood?"

She looked back at Niles' body and nodded.

"Good, give me your phone." Again she looked at me strange, but retrieved her purse off the dresser and took her phone out. Once I had it, I lifted Niles' phone from the nightstand and slid them both in my pocket. I didn't need her making any calls until our people had this place cleaned up, and that was going to take hours. So, until then, she was going to sit her ass in the corner and keep her damn mouth shut.

After our people had Niles' place cleaned up, Frank and I ran up on Sway. He was coming out of a club, so Frank walked up on him as he was about to get in his car and shot him in the head. We left him there because there was no need to worry about suspicion and it would look just like a random shooting. Frank had done some research and we also had the names of the two guys that did the actual shooting. Like most niggas, they couldn't keep their mouths closed, so they bragged about it. I guess it was a badge of honor to say that they shot

Theory Bryant. Oh well, that badge earned them a bullet in the head. Frank and I ditched the guns we used like we always did, and were prepared to head home to Rain and Diamond.

Both of us could breathe a little easier, but also understood that just because we handled this situation didn't mean that it would be the last. For now, we both planned on enjoying the concept of not having to look over our shoulders, at least for right now.

When we got to my house it was quiet, which meant that Rain and Diamond were asleep. It's almost two in the morning so I figured they would be.

"Yo', you might as well chill here tonight. It's late as fuck and I know you don't feel like heading out." I looked across at Frank after I reset the security system.

"Shit, I'm good with that. I got a bag in the truck since I planned on staying with Diamond anyway."

"You're awfully cozy for somebody who's just chillin'," I said, as I led the way upstairs.

"Mind ya damn business," Frank said and laughed. When we got to the top of the stairs, I pointed to the guest room across from us that had a light glow coming from it. We dapped each other and he headed that way, while I opened the door to my bedroom.

It was dark, but the closet light was on with the door pulled so that it was almost shut. I smiled because I knew that Rain didn't like to be alone and she damn sure didn't like to be in total darkness. She had been that way since we were kids and that hadn't changed. Even if I was next to her and she knew that she was safe in my arms, she still couldn't handle complete darkness. She said it reminded her of being in the basement of our group home because it was pitch black down there.

I walked over to her, tucked her hair behind her ear, and kissed her on her face. She mumbled my name and then pulled the covers up over her shoulder. That shit had me feeling some type of way. Damn, I was glad to have her in my bed, the thing that fucked with me the most though was that now that she was here, I knew that I had to have it like this every day. I would be all types of fucked up if I lost her again. I couldn't even consider that shit without my heart pounding. Rain broke me down in a way that made me vulnerable. I hated that because I knew that she was my weakness and it wouldn't take long for others to figure that out, too. I had to keep her safe; whatever that took, I was going to make it happen.

I shed my clothes and went straight to the bathroom. I had to wash the day off me before I got in bed with Rain and once I was done, I slid in next to her. Instinctively, she moved her body close to mine and wrapped her body around mine. I let my hands glide across her smooth, warm skin, and knew I was home. After I kissed her on the forehead and secured my arms around her, I closed my eyes and focused on the rhythm of her heartbeat. My mind began to settle and before long, I could feel sleep taking over, so I let go and let it.

-11-

Rain

I woke up with Theory's arm feeling heavy across my waist. I fit perfectly against his side with my leg resting across his thigh. I couldn't help, but smile about how normal this felt. I never had that sense of safety and comfort with anyone else, but with Theory, it was just effortless.

I really didn't want to move, but my bladder felt like it was about to explode, so I lifted his arm and inched away from his body. I kept looking back over my shoulder and he didn't budge. I knew that he was tired because it was late when he got in. I woke up briefly when I smelled his soap and felt his body next to mine, but then we were both out, just like that.

After I flushed and washed my hands, I grabbed my toothbrush and layered it with toothpaste, before shoving it in my mouth. I turned my back and leaned on the counter while I brushed my teeth and right before I was done, Theory pushed the door open, and walked in. He moved past me without speaking and then I heard him around the corner using the bathroom. Once he flushed, he rounded the corner, kissed me on the cheek, and then grabbed his toothbrush, still without saying a word.

I laughed. "Good morning to you, too."

Theory just glanced at me and finished brushing his teeth, so I left him there to go lay down again. A few minutes later he was next to me, with his arms around my body, kissing all over my face.

"Good morning," he mumbled, in between kisses.

"Oh, so now you can speak." I placed my hands on the side of his handsome face. His eyes were so intense when he looked at me, it was almost scary. It was like he was connecting with my soul.

"What?" Theory had a slight frown on his face.

"Nothing." I moved forward enough to peck his lips.

His frown got deeper. "You're looking at me like you want to say something." Theory's deep voice vibrated through my chest. He looked concerned, which made him look even sexier. His eyes were intense, while his jawline was tight, forcing his lips to purge together in a straight line. I just wanted to suck on them.

"I'm just happy. Nothing's wrong so stop looking like that." I couldn't hide the smile that was surfacing.

"I make you happy?" Theory pulled me closer to him before flipping me on my back. In no time at all, his hand was between my legs, while he used his knee to spread them wider for more access.

"Do I make you happy?" I asked, instead of answering him.

He lifted his head wearing a smirk before he lowered it again, sliding me shirt up with his free hand.

I felt his lips on my stomach and then down my thighs, before Theory lifted his body, grabbed the sides of my panties, yanking them down my legs.

"Hell yeah, I'm happy." His voice was muffled because he was planting kisses along my center, while applying pressure to my clit with his thumb. "You love me, Autumn Rain?"

I nodded because I didn't want to waste energy to open my mouth, even though I knew he couldn't see me. He was now roughly sucking my clit, while his hands had a tight grip on my thighs to hold them open.

"Rain, do you love me?"

I felt Theory's tongue flicking across my clit, and I was about to lose it so my answer came out strong and rushed. "Yes, please don't stop."

He laughed and dove in again like it was his last meal. This man had a way with my body like no other, because it only took minutes before I felt a warm sensations gushing out of me.

"You love this or me?" Theory asked, as he sat up to remove his clothes.

"Both," I answered truthfully, causing him to laugh, but that didn't last long because he ducked under my legs and entered me with so much force that I couldn't think straight. Theory was definitely not a small man, so it usually took me a minute to adjust, but he wasn't trying to hear that this morning.

I let out a deep breath so that I wouldn't pass out from holding it, while I held onto his arms, as he thrust inside me. Theory was hitting spots that I knew should have been off limits.

"Fuck, Rain, I can never get tired of this shit. It's like you were made just for me."

I felt his lips on my neck and then his teeth tugging at my skin. That had me motivated, so I started matching his strokes and before long, our bodies were in sync.

"Yes, Thee. I feel it coming." I yelled out, and then buried my face in his chest. He just laughed because he knew I was so damn close. My baby wanted me to have it just as much as I needed it, so his strokes got deeper and his hands slid under my ass to lift me just a little. That position caused his dick to rub roughly against my clit every time he moved in and out of me, so I lost it.

"Oh shit, I can't hold it anymore."

"My either, Rain, let that shit go and cum with me baby. Fuck."

We were both moaning and yelling so loud that I knew for sure if Frank and Diamond weren't already up, they were now.

After we were both able to breathe steady again, Theory rolled over onto his back and grabbed his chest.

"That shit right there needs to be illegal. I can't be doing this shit. You know my ass hasn't healed completely."

I slid my leg across his thighs, but he shoved it away. "Oh, hell no, I'm done ma. You gotta let my ass recover first."

I burst out laughing. "Oh, so you're tapping out?"

"Hell, yeah. I probably shouldn't have been doing that shit; got my body feeling all types of stress." Theory sat up and moved to the edge of the bed before looking back at me over his shoulder.

I sat up and crawled over to him, throwing my arms around his neck, and kissing the side of his face.

"It's all good. I still love you," I said, before I climbed around him and walked into the bathroom.

I could hear him laughing behind me. "Yeah, aight, talk shit now while my ass is only at fifty percent, but you know I got you, trust that."

I jumped in the shower and Theory joined me. We were both still worn out, so we actually just washed and got up. Once we were in the room again, I started getting dressed, but my back was to Theory, when I heard him ask me the most insane question.

"Why aren't you pregnant yet?" I turned to face him, but Theory was looking down at his waist tying the string to his joggers. I guess he felt my eyes on him because he looked up at me with the most serious expression.

"Because I'm on birth control. Why would you ask me that?" I know this fool didn't think we were about to have a baby.

"Stop taking it," he said, causally, like it didn't mean anything.

"No, I'm not doing that," I said, looking at him like he was crazy.

"Let me see it," he said, as he walked over to where I was standing.

"No, why?"

"Because I just want to see it," he said.

I turned to the dresser and reached in my purse to pull out my pack of pills. This idiot snatched it out my hand and put it in his pocket.

"Theory, stop playing. I'm not about to get pregnant, not now anyway."

"Why not? I have plenty of money and your ass better not be thinking that you're ever going to be with anyone else, so what else is there?"

I looked at him like he had lost his mind.

"There's a hell of a lot more to it. We haven't even figured things out with us and did you not just have someone shooting at you. I'm not raising a child by myself, Theory."

"Ain't shit gonna happen to me, you should know that by now, and the fuck you mean we haven't figured things out with us? This shit right here is figured out," he pointed at me, and then himself.

"It's not that simple Thee, and you know it. Do you even really want a kid? A baby changes everything."

"Changes everything like what, you're still gonna be you, and I'm still gonna be me? We'll just have a miniature us to add to the picture, and hell yeah I want a kid. I wouldn't have said that shit if I didn't. Don't you?"

"I do but—"

"But what, Rain? You either do or you don't. You don't trust me? You don't think I'll be here for you? I'm not going anywhere and this shit right there with us, this is it. For me anyway, and I hope this is it for you, too."

"It is and you know that."

"Then, what the fuck else is there? You wanna get married? Shit, we can go buy a damn ring right now; whatever the fuck you want, but I want a baby Rain, with you. Just you, so you're not taking this shit anymore."

He reached in his pocket and held up my pills before he placed them on the dresser. He looked at them and then me, before he left the room, and I stood there trying to figure out what just happened.

After I dressed, I made my way to the kitchen where I found Frank and Theory, deep in conversation, at the table. Diamond was standing in front of the stove handling an oversized frying pan, with what looked like eggs in it.

"Hey, boo, you don't mind, do you?" Diamond nodded towards the pan she had on the stove.

"Nah, you're good." I walked over to the refrigerator to retrieve a pack of bacon before she got the baking sheet from under the cabinet, and started laying the strips down.

Diamond followed my lead and started the oven.

"Good morning, Rain," Frank said, from across the room. I was so stuck on Theory and his damn demand about having a baby that I didn't realize that I hadn't spoken to everyone.

"Morning Frank, you look happy," I said, and then cut my eyes at Diamond, before focusing on Frank, again.

He chuckled before he stole a glance at Diamond. "I might be."

Diamond balled up her fist and nailed me in my arm. "Mind your business."

"What's up, ma, you don't want her to know how I put it down last night?" Frank said, now focused on Diamond.

She looked over her shoulder and rolled her eyes before she looked at me and whispered, "Laid that shit down, boo," and then offered a grin.

"You so damn extra," I said, and then laughed.

"Nah, boo, extra was your ass this morning," Diamond said, and then glanced at the guys to see if they were paying attention.

My eyes got wide and I threw my hand over my mouth and laughed. "Damn, did you hear that?"

"Thin walls boo, but it's all good."

"My damn walls ain't thin, her ass just can't handle this dick," Theory said, with a smirk.

I shot him a bird and then moved Diamond out the way so that I could put the bacon in the oven.

"It's all good, boo, we're grown," Diamond snickered, and then dumped the eggs she was scrambling on to a plate that she had on the counter next to her.

"Trust me, I know, and he knows that's a damn lie," I said. I could hear Theory chuckling behind me.

"What's the move for the day? It's Saturday and I want to do something fun," Diamond said.

"Me too." We both turned to look at the guys.

"What's fun?" Theory asked.

"I don't know… anything… we can just hang out today. Hit the mall, go eat, anything, other than sit up in this house," I said.

Frank laughed, "Ain't shit fun about going to the mall."

"It is, if I'm with you," Diamond said, offering him a seductive smile.

"Man, forget that shit, I don't care who the fuck is with me. Ain't shit fun about being at a mall," Frank said, causing Diamond to roll her eyes and the rest of us to laugh. "But you can get that though, with your sexy ass," he winked at her.

"Yo', chill with all that shit. I know I already need to fumigate my damn guest room with your nasty asses," Theory said, mugging Frank.

Frank just laughed, "That's her," he said, pointing at Diamond.

"Both y'all asses are nasty. Did you wash your hands before you started making those?" I said, pointing to the plate of eggs.

"Yes, hoe, I ain't that damn nasty. Did you wash your damn hands? Don't forget I heard you screaming this morning, too."

"She's good, that was all me this morning. She didn't have to touch shit, just bend over and take it."

Theory was now biting his bottom lip, which had me wanting to say fuck breakfast, time for round two.

"And y'all call us nasty," Diamond said, frowning at me.

"How about we discuss our plans for the day. This shit is getting weird. Grown or not, I don't wanna hear about what he fuck y'all got going on," Frank said.

Theory laughed. "True, y'all figure that shit out, because I know we don't get a vote," he pointed at me and Diamond, blew me a kiss, and then turned to finish his conversation with Frank.

After breakfast and everyone was dressed, we split into two separate vehicles and headed towards downtown Atlanta. Diamond and I wanted to check out a few boutiques before we hit the mall. Theory and Frank were with us, but off into their own worlds, while we shopped, until we actually hit the mall. The four of us walked around, hand in hand, looking relationship perfection, unless Diamond and I were trying on, or purchasing stuff.

After everyone was satisfied and ready to leave, we decided to hit up Olive Garden for a late lunch. It didn't take long for us to be seated at our table and everyone was quite in their own space, while we surveyed the menus.

"Man, I'm so hungry everything looks good. I could literally get one of everything," I said, more to myself than anybody in general.

Theory laughed. "You don't eat shit, so I know that's a lie, but all that's gonna change when you carrying my shorty."

I looked up at him like he was crazy. First of all, because he wouldn't let this baby thing go and secondly, because he said that out loud in front of Diamond and Frank.

"Shorty?" Diamond asked. "We having a baby?"

I said "no" and Theory said "yes," but we spoke at the same time.

"You know it takes two to make that ship happen?" Frank said, joining in.

"Trust me, I know that. I don't know why she's tripping," Theory said, looking right at me like his request, or rather demand, was simple.

"Awe boo, do it. You two would make a pretty baby. Y'all so cute."

"If you say that one more damn time," I said, narrowing my eyes at Diamond. She laughed and shrugged.

"You see that; they agree," Theory said.

"Oh, hell no, don't put me in that shit. I didn't agree to a damn thing. I'm not in it," Frank said.

"Damn, nigga, it will be your god child, not your actual child. You don't have to do a damn thing, but buy shit and play with them. You acting like you'll have to raise my shorty," Theory laughed.

"Aight then, do that shit. I can get with that."

Theory leaned over and kissed me on the cheek. See, they agree."

"Yeah, well they don't have to carry a baby for nine months and then wake up in the middle of the night when it's screaming its head off.'

"That's what the fuck you worried about?" Theory looked at me and frowned.

"No, but that's part of it. It will be *my* baby." Everybody was all in when the baby talk started, but when it was all said and done, it was the mother who got stuck handling all things baby related.

"Don't play me like that Rain. You know I'm not that person and that's fucked up that you would say some shit like that." I could tell that I pissed him off.

Honestly, I could handle having a baby with Theory because I knew that he would cherish and protect our child, the same way he protected me. It just wasn't that simple in my head.

I reached for Theory's hand and at first he snatched his away from me, but the second time I reached for it, he let me. I laced my fingers through his and he looked down at me and smiled, before leaning in to peck me on the lips.

"If it happens, it happens." That simple statement caused his smile to grow wider, before he grabbed my chin and hit me with a deeper kiss.

"Aye, all is right in the world. The happy couple is having a baby," Diamond said, smiling at us with a goofy ass grin.

"Kiss my ass, hoe," I said, and then rolled my eyes at her while she just laughed.

After everyone ordered and our food arrived, we all ate and talked for the next hour, before we decided to head our separate ways. The day had been almost perfect, but once we made our way to the parking, our perfectly good day did a one-eighty, after we all laid eyes on, Destiny. *Oh shit, here we go.*

-12-

Diamond

"Is this why you won't return my call?" Destiny walked up to me, getting right in my face, so I shoved her back. I knew it was just a matter of time before she saw me out somewhere with Frank. Today was not the day, though.

Destiny laughed after she regained her balance. "I guess that's my answer right there." She was looking right at Frank. My eyes moved from him to Theory, and then Rain, who moved right behind me like she was ready to jump on Destiny, if needed. I would have smiled if this psycho bitch wasn't standing in front of me.

"I haven't returned your calls because I don't want to talk to your crazy ass. It don't have shit to do with him, but trust me, he is motivation to keep it that way." I pointed my finger right in her face so that it grazed her forehead, but she reached up and slapped it away.

Destiny laughed. "Yeah, well that won't last for long, will it? Never does." She wore a pleased smirk, again, looking at Frank.

"How about you let me worry about that. My relationship with him is none of your damn business. Whether we make it or not, trust me when I say I will not be fucking with you ever again. You don't understand boundaries and your ass needs to be locked up somewhere in a white coat. Now, if you'll excuse me, I would like to enjoy the rest of my day." I turned to walk away and this crazy hoe grabbed my hair and yanked me back, but before I could turn to do anything, I felt Rain fly by me. Next thing I knew, Destiny let me go. When I could actually see her, she was holding her eye and about to lunge at Rain, but Theory stepped in-between them.

"Look ma, I don't know what beef you got and I really don't give a fuck, but you damn sure not about to put your hands on her. Your shit swelling already, so if I were you I would go tend to that," he said, holding Rain behind him with one arm, while Frank moved beside him. I could see Frank out the corner of my eye and he was pissed.

"You know what? You can get that, but trust me, if I see your ass again, be ready."

Rain laughed. "Bitch, just make sure it's not anytime soon so it will be a fair fight. Right now your ass is handicapped with only one eye."

I didn't want to laugh, but I couldn't help it, and Destiny looked right at me. "Oh, so that shit is funny to you? When his dick gets old, your ass won't be laughing when you're begging for my attention again," Destiny said, and then walked back to her car, instead of going in the restaurant.

"Damn, I guess we ruined her appetite," Rain said, with a grin.

I just shook my head and laughed, "You need to stop."

"You know you wrong for hitting that girl like that. I don't know why you think you can just put your hands on people lately," Theory said, grinning at Rain.

She shrugged. "I owed Diamond."

Theory looked at her strangely, but I knew she was referring to the time I got my hands on Alex the day we ran into her, kicking it with Mel.

"Yo', I'm out." Frank's voice caught me off guard. He glanced at me before he dapped Theory, and then said goodbye to Rain. Without another word, he started walking to his truck. When he reached it, he walked to the passenger side, opened the door and then walked around and got in the driver's side, slamming the door.

We all looked at him and Theory's eyes were on me. "Don't worry about him, he'll be alright. And if he keeps that shit up, call me and I'll handle him for you," Theory smiled, but I could tell he knew Frank well enough to know that he was about to be on this for a minute.

"We're good, we just have some things to talk about." I hugged Rain, and then offered her and Theory both a forced smile.

"Call me later, boo."

"I will," I said, before I started towards Frank's truck.

An ex showing their ass, was still an ex showing their ass, regardless of gender. But I knew that with this situation, Frank was more worried about the fact that it was Destiny, versus the fact that she was acting like a psycho maniac.

When I reached Frank's truck, I got in and shut the door. He didn't look at me, nor did he say a word. In fact, he just pulled off, damn near throwing my body into the passenger window, from how he wwhipped out of the spot he was in, and rounded the row of cars that we moved past.

"You going to talk to me or just keep driving like you don't have any damn sense, trying to give me a concussion?" I looked right at Frank and he offered up the hardest stare, but only for about five seconds before he chuckled, and then focused on the road again. His hand moved to the volume of the radio and once it came blasting through his speakers, he pressed the gas to increase his speed.

I see he wanted to be in his feelings for a minute. I decided to give him that until we got where we were going, but his ass was going to talk to me. I looked around trying to figure out what direction we were driving in because I honestly didn't have a clue. Before I could really focus on it though, I heard my phone go off with a text notification. So, I leaned down to get it out my purse. While I read the message from Rain, I could feel Frank watching me, but I wasn't going to give him the satisfaction, so I stayed focused on my phone. If he wanted to know who it was, all he had to do was open his damn mouth, and ask.

Aye, boo. You good. Frank seemed pissed.

Yeah, I'm straight Layla, but he's in his damn feelings

Layla?? And he'll get over it that was insane

Layla Ali lol, yeah it was but he can't take that shit out on me so he better get over it!!

You're so damn stupid but that hoe had it coming. Theory told me I need to learn how to keep my damn hands to myself lol. Don't worry about Frank, just give him a minute.

I'm not worried about him. Hell I'm with him and I told that bitch to kick rocks. So he better tighten up but let me go before I have to smack his ass

You need back up? Lol

Bye fool, your ass hit two hoes and you think you hard lol

Aye, I'm down for my team lol

I smiled, locked my screen and dropped my phone in my lap. I could feel Frank burning a hole in the side of my face, so I looked up at him.

"What?" I dished out as much attitude as I could.

Frank released a sarcastic laugh under his breath, but still didn't say anything. "Okay fine, you wanna play this game? I'm the queen of petty." I picked up my phone again, unlocked it and started typing in my notes. I wasn't texting a damn soul, but he didn't know that. I made sure to laugh and show plenty of teeth, and he was heated. By the time we pulled up at my complex, I knew he was ready to explode, but like I said, I was queen of petty, so I was good.

"I've got a few things to do." Frank looked at me like he was waiting for me to get out, which threw me. I thought for sure he would at least want to come in and talk. Damn, now what?

When my eyes fell on him I wanted to smile because he looked so damn sexy. I could see the anger in his dark brown eyes, that housed a slight slant. His full lips formed a straight line because his jaw was tight. With one arm propped up on the windowsill, while his hand rested on the steering wheel, I could clearly trace the definition in his muscles. His other hand reached up and scratched his freshly cut hair, before his hand went across it and then stopped at the nape of his neck.

"Fine." As much as I wanted to break, I wasn't going to. My ass was too damn stubborn and none of this was my fault.

Frank let out a frustrated breath before he lowered his head briefly, and then looked up at me. I pulled my purse up over my shoulder and reached for the door handle.

"What the fuck am I supposed to do with that shit Dia?" He called me by my nickname, so I could tell he was coming down off his adrenaline rush.

"Do with what Frank?" I turned to look at him, but his eyes were focused straight ahead.

He chuckled and then looked me right in my eyes. "Don't play dumb, Diamond. You know what the fuck I'm talking about."

"Unless you plan on cheating on me with her, then you don't need to do shit with that." I made sure to keep my expression neutral.

Frank laughed sarcastically, and shook his head. "Get out my damn truck with that childish bullshit, and when you want to have an adult conversation, you call me."

The way Frank looked at me had me rethinking my smart ass comment. I didn't want him to leave.

"I'm just saying, you're asking me what you're supposed to do with the whole Destiny thing. You don't need to do a damn thing with it, and neither do I. I'm with you and that's all that matters.

"Yeah, well she obviously don't believe that." Frank let his head fall back on the seat and closed his eyes. I could tell he was annoyed, but now he seemed more concerned about the situation, than mad.

"I don't care what she believes. You can see I wasn't entertaining her bullshit so that should tell you something." I reached for Frank's hand, but he snatched it away and turned his head just enough to look at me.

"That's your life so I know you don't get this shit, but try to see it from my perspective. I'm not worried about another nigga; never have been and never will be. I know what I'm fucking with so that shit don't faze me, but this shit right here, I can't get with. How the fuck am I supposed compete with that shit?"

"Who says you have to?"

"You were with her ass for a reason Diamond, so she obviously was giving your ass something you wanted."

My mouth fell open before it closed and opened again, but I really had no clue what to say, so I didn't say anything.

"Exactly, you figure that shit out and then you come talk to me. I'll get up with you later. I need to go take care of a few things."

My pride was hurt and I knew that there wasn't really anything that I could say, so I just pulled the handle and got out.

Frank waited for me to walk towards my apartment, but I stopped by the door and just watched him. After a few minutes, he let the window down and I heard his voice.

"Go inside so that I can leave, Dia." Now I was in my feelings. He was leaving, but he wanted to make sure I was okay before he did. That made me want him even more and I knew I couldn't have him, not right now, anyway.

When I didn't move, once again, he let out a frustrated breath and I noticed his hand reach for his forehead as he massaged his temple.

"Diamond, please go inside; I got some shit to do."

Defeated, I just turned towards my door and used my key to unlock it. Once I was inside, I went straight to the window and caught Frank, just as he was pulling off. I guess that was that. I dropped my stuff on the sofa and started removing my clothes, letting them fall to the floor as I made my way to my bedroom. I felt a good nap on the horizon. I didn't really want to think about Frank, or Destiny, and the only way that was happening was if I could shut my brain off. Even if it was temporary, I was about to erase the day, or at least the end of it.

13

Frank

I had been driving around for hours with no real destination. I just couldn't get that shit out my head and it was really starting to fuck with me. I wasn't the type to fall for a female that quick, and truth be told, there were only two women in my life that really ever had my heart, my mother and my ex. My mother passed two years ago of a heart attack and my ex, well she was a special case. I royally fucked up with her and lost her, but to this day she and I remained close. Rachel and I were good friends, maybe the best of friends, but she was married with kids, and all because I was too young and stupid to realize that no amount of available pussy, was worth losing your heart. Lesson learned though, and now I have to see Rachel living the life that she should have had with me, with another nigga. It was cool, though. I had respect for him; shit, he caught me slipping and became the man to Rachel, that I was too childish to be.

Thinking about Rachel made me want to talk to her, so I dialed her up and hoped that she wasn't on some family type shit. I made a point of never making waves in her personal life. It was the least I could do, since I was the reason why she moved on.

"Damn, that's eerie as hell. I was just thinking about you." Rachel's voice flowed through my phone and I couldn't help but smile when she let out a soft chuckle.

"Word, what were you thinking?"

"Just wondering how you were doing. I haven't talked to you in a minute." I could hear a hint of disappointment in her voice, but I decided to let that ride.

"Shit, you know me, I've just been chillin'. What about you, you good, though?"

"I'm good, Frank. These damn kids are making me question my sanity, but other than that, I'm good," she laughed, almost to herself, as if she were sharing a private joke.

I sat there processing the fact that she had kids with another nigga.

"Frank?"

The sound of her voice moved my focus back to our conversation. "Yeah, I bet, but you love that shit, though."

"I do, couldn't see my life any other way." I could hear the smile in her voice and it cut deep. I low-key missed when I used to be the only one she could see her life with. "What about you Frank, what's up? I can tell you got something on your mind."

"I'm good, just wanted to call and say what's up. Nothing else," I lied. Even though I knew she didn't mind, I didn't feel right talking to her about my personal situation.

"Frank, talk to me. We're friends, right?"

I laughed. "Yeah we're friends, but I'm sure you don't want to hear about my bullshit personal problems."

"If you need to talk then I'll listen, you know that," she said.

It took me a minute, but I figured what the hell. "So, I've been kicking it with this shorty for a minute and she's cool as hell. We vibe something serious and I can see myself making something out of this."

"That doesn't sound like a bullshit problem to me." Rachel sounded confused.

"Her ex is the bullshit part of this equation."

"He's not letting go?" Rachel asked.

"She."

"She doesn't want to let go of her ex? Well sounds like y'all not vibing like you think then," Rachel laughed.

"Nah, I mean she, as in her ex is a she."

I held the phone, waiting.

"Oh, so it's like that?" Rachel asked.

"You see my dilemma?"

"What's she saying about the situation?"

"She claims she's not going back, but fuck, I've never dealt with anything like this. Another nigga I can handle because that shit don't faze me. My dick game is all that, but I can't fuck with another female. I don't even know how that shit works."

Rachel laughed.

"The fuck you laughing for?" I asked, a little irritated.

"I'm laughing at your dumb ass. Niggas always think good dick is enough. I left you and your bomb ass dick game, didn't I?" Rachel snapped, catching me off guard. She paused and continued. "Good dick will only get you so far, Frank. What else are you giving her? Women want time and attention. They want to know that they're a priority, and not an option. The simple things like the streets, your boys, and other women, will never affect their importance in your life. Another woman can relate to that and understand that. I mean it's not my thing, but I can see how she might roll that way."

I could tell that Rachel was hitting me with her feelings about what I didn't give her, but there was an honesty in it that related directly to Diamond. It was just hard for her not to connect the two.

"I don't do all that bitch shit Rachel, you know me."

She laughed a little too hard for my liking. "You're so damn stupid. I can see not much has changed. You're not being a bitch if you make sure your woman knows that she's a priority to you, Frank. Emotions don't make you soft, they make you whole, and a real man can balance his sensitive side, with his masculine one."

"I guess that's why you left my ass for that nigga you call yourself with now, huh?" I teased.

"Something like that, but that's not what we're talking about. You feeling her right?"

"Yeah, she cool."

"You want something solid with her?"

"You plan on leaving that nigga anytime soon?"

"Frank, I'm serious." I could hear the annoyance in her voice.

"Yeah, I want this shit to work."

"Then, don't worry about her past. If she's not giving you any reason to think that she's going back, then don't worry about it. But I do want to meet the woman that has you calling me to figure out how to connect with your feelings. She must be something serious," Rachel laughed, but I could hear the undertone of jealousy hidden beneath it.

"Yeah, she's serious. She's not you, you already know that, but I'm feeling her."

"Don't do that. That's not fair to her."

I chuckled. "How you gonna take her side. You a damn trip, Rach."

"I'm a woman and I know my feelings would be all types of fucked up if I knew my so-called man was comparing me to another female."

"Nah, I'm not doing that. There's only one you. I fucked that up and have to live with it, but you right, I'll figure it out. But let me let you get back to your happily married life."

This time Rachel laughed. "I miss you, Frank. Regardless of what you think, I'll always have love for you, but now it's time for you to work on your own happily married life. You deserve to be happy and if this chick will be that for you, then make it work. But trust me, if she's on some bullshit, I'll fuck her up for you."

I laughed so hard I damn near choked myself. "Oh, so you gonna fuck up my girl if she don't act right? I don't think that nigga of yours would appreciate that, Rach."

"You're right, but I'll do that just for you."

"'Preciate that. Take care Rach and I'll take to you soon."

"Fix it, Frank… You obviously care, so find a way to make it work."

"Yeah, aight."

I ended the call and looked at Rachel's house. I had driven there while we were talking and was parked across the street. I noticed a light on in their living room and wondered if that's where she was. Didn't matter though; that part of my life was over and I respected her too much to disrupt what she had. I inhaled and let it out slowly, before I started my truck and pulled away from the curb. I needed to go talk to Diamond and figure out my next move.

*****

"You gonna stand there looking at me or can I come in?" I watched Diamond's face and she looked annoyed, but I could tell she wanted to smile because I was there. It was late as hell, because I drove around the city for a few more hours before I was ready to have this conversation with her.

Diamond didn't say a word, she just removed her hand from her apartment door and walked away. My eyes were glued to her ass, which was spilling out the bottom of the boy cut panties she was wearing. I shut her door and locked it, before following her down the hall, towards her bedroom. Rain was with Theory, so we were alone, which was a good thing.

After I reached Diamond's bedroom, I stood in the doorway leaning against the frame, and watched as she climbed into her bed. Once her back was against the headboard, she reached for her comforter, pulling it up around her waist. She let her hands rest in her lap, before her eyes focused on me.

Damn, she was sexy as hell. Her lips slightly poked out, sitting pretty on her oval face. I really wanted to just kiss her. Diamond had rich chocolate skin, but it was smooth as hell, and flawless. Her eyes were not really hazel, but still a lighter shade of brown. She had a set of thick eyebrows that were always perfectly trimmed. She claimed it was natural, but them shits were too perfect not to be manicured. She was truly beautiful, with the personality to match. Diamond was funny as hell and you never knew what to expect when she opened her mouth. I loved that about her. I couldn't stand a woman that was uptight, and didn't know how to relax and just go with the flow.

"Well?" she said, breaking my thoughts about her.

"Well, what?

"You're here, so you must have something to say," she said, refusing to break eye contact with me.

Her little feisty ass had my dick hard already.

"Maybe you're the one who needs to have something to say," I said, making sure I didn't really show any emotions. Hell, at this point I wasn't even stressed about that shit anymore. I just wanted to fuck her and go to sleep.

"I said everything I needed to say. I was with her, now I'm with you and unless you plan on being with someone else, then that's not changing for me."

I chuckled and stepped in her room. When I was next to the side of the bed that she was on I stopped, folded my arms, and looked down at her, with a smirk.

"It's that easy, huh?"

"Why wouldn't it be? I'm not a damn child, Frank. I don't need to play games. I want you or I wouldn't be here."

"Yes, the fuck you would, you live here," I said, just to fuck with her.

"You're so damn childish; you know what I mean."

"So, you want me Diamond?"

"Did I fucking stutter?"

Here she goes. "That smart ass mouth of yours is about to have you in trouble."

She sucked her teeth and rolled her eyes. "Whatever."

"Don't make me regret this shit because I don't give second chances. I mean that." I made sure she could see how serious I was.

"Neither do I," she returned, making me laugh.

"This ain't about you though, and I don't put my hands on females, but if that bitch gets out of line again, I'm gonna let Rain fuck her up."

Diamond looked up at me and laughed. "Yeah, well, me and you both."

She climbed out of her bed and stood in front of me, leaving only inches between us. Her hands moved under my shirt before she grabbed the sides and attempted to move it up my body, to get it off. I could smell the vanilla scent that clung to her skin and it made my mouth water. I wanted to taste her.

"Are we done with this?" she asked, after I reached behind my back to help remove my shirt.

I looked down as her hands moved to my belt buckle. "I guess so, since you trying to get me naked and shit."

"Break up, to make up." She looked up at me with a grin before l leaned down and kissed her. I could spend hours kissing, and sucking on her lips. They were so soft and sweet every time I made contact with them; one of the things that I loved about her.

"I didn't break up with your ass, so you better have been here alone while I was gone."

A smirk spread across her face. "Maybe."

I grabbed her chin and looked right in her eyes before my lips found hers, again. "Don't fucking play. Trust me, that's not the move right now."

Once our clothes were on her floor, I grabbed her around the waist, lifting her enough for her legs to wrap around me. I lowered her onto her dresser and felt her hands grip my dick, stroking it for a minute, before she positioned it at her opening, but I waited there for a minute, making eye contact.

"If we're in this, then we're really in this." My statement was simple, but it meant a lot. I had no plans to do any type of back and forth with Diamond, and I damn sure wasn't about to do any type of drama. If I was man enough to put her first and make her the only person in my life, then I needed to be sure that she was returning the favor.

"I'm in this if you are." I could tell from the way Diamond looked at me that she meant what she said, so I had to go with that for now. It was no guarantee that it wouldn't change, but for now, we were good.

My lips found hers and I kissed her so deeply that I felt my dick getting harder every time my tongue danced against hers. I still hadn't entered her yet, but she was damn sure was trying to make it happen. My head was at her opening and Diamond kept scooting her body closer to the edge of her dresser, which made me laugh, because her impatient ass was going to hit the floor if she moved any closer.

I stopped fighting it and slid inside her, almost losing it. She was dripping wet, tight as fuck and with every inch I progressed, she tightened her muscles, damn near making it difficult to move further. Fuck that, I grabbed her ass and pulled her into me and when I hit rock bottom, her voice filled the room.

"Oh, shit." I smiled and proceeded with a slow steady stroke, but my pace gradually picked up. I wanted her to understand what she had and that I wasn't to be played with.

"Why you trying to get away now, Dia. Your ass was about to die for me to enter you a minute ago." I bit down on her neck when I felt her hand slide between us. She kept trying to push me away, but I wasn't having no parts of that.

The deeper I went, the more she whimpered and begged me for mercy.

"Frank, slow down. You're gonna make me cum too fast." Diamond's breathing was labored and she could barely get the words out.

I looked at her and laughed. "That's the point ain't it? Let that shit go, ma; you know I got you."

She looked at me and shook her head before she grabbed the back of my neck and tugged on my bottom lip, before she began sucking it. She knew what she was doing. She wanted me to cum with her. I could already feel it building. I held Diamond closer to me and started working her body with so much force and passion that she couldn't talk, because her ass could barely breathe. She was mumbling and moaning, but that shit was cute as hell. Problem was, it was making me go harder, and I wasn't ready to bust, but I couldn't stop it. Diamond was so wet, I could hear all types of sounds fill the room every time out bodies collided, so I stopped fighting it, and let it happen. After a few more strong strokes, we both screamed out at the same time. If her neighbors didn't know she was fucking, they damn sure knew it now.

"Damn, Frank, you trying to make a point." Diamond looked at me, breathing hard, and with a frown on her face.

She looked so serious I couldn't hide my smile. "Nah, ma, why you say that?" I was still holding her in place and our bodies were pressed together, while I was still inside her. I started kissing and sucking on her neck because I was ready for round two, and knew it wouldn't take much to get me there.

"Oh, hell no, I need a minute." Diamond leaned back and narrowed her eyes at me. "First last night and now tonight; you're trying to break something in there.

"I thought that's what you wanted," I said, in-between kisses. I could already feel my dick getting hard again, so I started sliding in and out of her, slowly as I grew.

"Frank," Diamond whined, holding her stomach.

"What Dia, don't tell me you can't take this dick? You just agreed that we're in this. You know what that means. This is my shit and I want it right now." My eyes met hers and she looked like she was about to cry.

I lifted her off the dresser and carried her to the bed, making sure I stayed inside of her the entire time.

Once her back was on the bed, I positioned my weight on my arms and looked down at her.

"I got you, ma."

With slow, steady strokes, I plunged in and out of her, making sure I was gentle enough for her to take it. For the second night in a row, I had worked her little ass out, so right now I was going to give her a pass. I'd murder her pussy another day. I buried my face in her neck and did something I hadn't done in a long ass time, I made love to my woman.

14

Rain

"Are you taking me to work?" I bent down to tie my Converse and then stood up to walk into the closet, where Theory was.

"Nah, but Bull's on his way." Theory said it so casually that I almost believed him, until he turned to face me with a smirk.

"You better be glad you're playing because I wasn't going anywhere with him."

"You were if I said you were." Theory moved past me, but not before stopping to kiss my lips. The smell of his cologne tickled my nose and trailed behind him as he left the closet, so I followed. Once I was in front of the dresser, I lifted my brush and began maneuvering my hair into a high ponytail. I didn't really feel like doing much to it and we didn't have any assignments. That meant I didn't have to leave the office, or worry about meeting clients, so a ponytail was going for today.

"So, does that mean that you're taking me?" I asked, after I had my hair secured.

"I will if you want me to, but you can drive."

I watched Theory's face trying to read his mood. If I could drive myself; that meant that the threat was gone.

"You took care of Niles?" I asked.

Theory's expression let me know that my question surprised him. "We'll talk about it."

"Don't look at me like that. I know what you do and I knew what you were going to have to do."

Theory looked at me with a cocky grin before he reached for me, pulling me onto his lap, after he sat on the bed.

"Oh yeah, and what is it that I do?" I could hear the playfulness in his voice.

"I'm not stupid, Thee."

"I know that, but check it. That part of my life is changing. I was actually making moves to get out before you even showed up, but especially now. After all that went down, I had to put that on hold for a minute, but I'm getting out. My detail shops will be it for me."

My legs were across his lap, so I was turned partially towards him. "Does it even work like that?"

Theory looked at me and I could tell he was trying to choose his words carefully. "I mean, truthfully, I'll be connected to this shit for life and I'll be there for Frank with whatever he needs, but I'm distancing myself from it."

I shrugged, "I'm good with whatever. As long as I know you got me, I'm good."

Theory's eyes fell on mine and then he chuckled. "Oh, so you're my little rider now, huh?"

I smiled and kissed him. "I'm your everything because I better be all you got."

"Just remember you said that shit when I need you to make these runs for me." Theory smacked the side of my thigh, and lifted me so that he could stand.

"I'm not saying all that," I said, before I walked out the room and I could hear him right behind me.

"Nah, you're in this shit, now. You can't punk out on me, Autumn Rain."

I just shook my head and laughed. Honestly, I would be whatever he needed me to be. I loved him that much and he knew it. The difference was that Theory would never put me in that position because he loved me even more. That was just how we worked.

*****

"So, tell me what happened. Your lying ass didn't call me last night." I walked into Diamond's office and plopped down in one of the chairs that sat in front of her desk.

"Damn, you nosy." Diamond looked up from her laptop with a grin and leaned back in her chair, placing her elbows up on the arms of it. She was smiling like a little kid, but I could tell it didn't have anything to do with my comment.

"Yeah, well I learned from the best. You wanted a friend now you got one, so spill it, hoe." I playfully rolled my eyes and then blew her a kiss.

"Oh, so that's how we're doing it?" Diamond laughed and then looked down at her phone, which was going off. Whatever she was looking at made her smile even harder. She picked her phone up, but I stood and snatched it out of her hands.

"Frank can wait, but I see y'all fixed things from the way your ass is over there grinning."

Diamond reached for her phone, but I held it behind my back. I needed details before she started ignoring me, to talk to Frank.

"Talk first and then you can finish sexting, with your nasty ass."

"Okay, and when Frank shows up here acting crazy because I ignored his text, I'm pointing straight to your nosey ass."

"Girl, bye, ain't nobody worried about Frank."

"Yeah, alright, just remember you said that," Diamond laughed. "But we're good though. When we left the restaurant he dropped me off at my apartment and then left, all in his feelings. He was gone most of the night, but then came back later, acting like nothing happened. All he really said was that if we're in this, then we're in this, and that he doesn't give second chances."

She looked at me and shrugged.

"Hoe, that can't be it."

"It really is, though," she laughed. "I mean, he tried to blow my back out to stress the point that he was the king of my castle, but other than that, that was it."

I could tell from the look on her face that she was reminiscing about her late night activities, so I shook my head, and tossed her phone back to her. Of course, she went right in, texting Frank and grinning like a teenager in love.

"So, what's up with the baby thing, boo? Seems like it's more his idea, than yours." Diamond had finished her text to Frank and was now focused on me, again.

"I don't know what's up with that. It's not like we ever talked about it, so that just threw me." I could feel my face turning into a frown.

"He almost died, Rain. I bet that put a lot of things into perspective." Diamond's expression grew serious like she was connecting with how Theory was likely processing things.

"Yeah, I thought about that, too. I just don't want to rush things. It's not like a puppy and I don't want to have a baby and then he realizes that it's not the life he wanted."

"Girl, please. I don't know much about Theory and I've only known him for a hot minute, but that man knows what he wants. If he said it, believe it. But, what do you want?"

Without even thinking about it my hand covered my stomach. "I can see it."

"Yeah, hoe, you can obviously feel it, too." Diamond glanced at my hand and we both laughed, as my phone went off. I pulled it out of my back pocket and realized that it was an unsaved number, so I scrunched up my faced, but answered.

"Is this Rain?"

Now, I was really looking crazy. I didn't know the number, but the sexy ass voice sounded familiar, I just couldn't place it.

"Who's this?" I asked, before admitting my identity.

He chuckled. "My bad baby girl, this is Jax. Charlotte gave me your number. I hope that's alright?"

"Depends on what you needed it for." Now I was really curious. I looked up and mouthed Jax to Diamond because I could tell she was dying to know who I was talking to. As soon as I said his name, she leaned forward, propping her elbows up, and lowering her chin into her hands.

"I need a favor."

"Umm, okay. What's up?"

"I know you weren't really feeling the whole album release thing, but I really want you there. I need press there… well, press that I can trust, and you and Diamond did your thing. It's not really an article type situation, but I know you guys are a team, so I want her there too. Detroit is trying to put me with some bullshit dude named, Hanson, and I'm not fucking with him like that. The first time we met, he was more worried about Charlotte, than me. I'm not really feeling that and I might have to fuck him up for doing some fucked shit. I don't need any bad press right now, so I would really appreciate it if you would handle it for me."

He waited and I sat there processing. I knew for sure Detroit was going to be there, which meant that his stupid ass daughter would probably be there. I wanted to lay hands on the bitch, but not at an album release party.

"I just don't know if that's a good idea."

"Look, I know you weren't feeling Detroit, and I'm not sure what's going on with that, but I promise I'll keep him away from you. You don't have to stay all night, just long enough to do some press photos for me. I know they'll be plenty of others there, but I trust you and I know you'll make sure I'm good. Charlotte will be there too, and maybe that will give you two a chance to catch up. I don't know what the deal is with her either, but she talks about you a lot. She misses you, Rain."

I had a lot to think about with Detroit, Lani, and Charlotte, but he was damn near begging me and his sexy ass voice was making it hard to say no.

"Fine, we'll be there, but only for a little while. As far as Charlotte and I, we'll see, but you owe me, big time," I teased.

He laughed and it was too damn sexy. *Oh Lord, panty wetter*. Loving Theory didn't control my ability to recognize sexy. I didn't want Jax in any way whatsoever, but it didn't hide the fact that I knew Jax sounded sexy as hell on the phone. "I got you, ma. Whatever, whenever."

I ended the call and looked right at Diamond. "We're going to Jax's album release party."

"How the fuck did that happen, and why is he calling you personally? Theory is going to fuck him up, and you, too, especially if your ass don't stop looking like you're about to have an orgasm over there," Diamond said with a grin.

"Girl, please. I'm happy with my situation, but his ass did sound sexy as hell."

"Yeah, well you better get that in check and how did he get your number anyway?"

I laughed, "Charlotte gave it to him."

"Oh hell, not only is Theory gonna fuck you up, but your damn sister, too. I know good and damn well by the way she was clinging to that man that she didn't just offer up your number. He went through her phone and got that shit." Diamond had a smug look on her face.

"Please stop, trust me, there is nothing there. In fact, he was trying to get me to spend time with Charlotte."

"Yeah, hoe, so he can have easy access to you," Diamond laughed. I just shook my head.

"I'm going to get some work done. How 'bout you stop sexting Frank and follow my lead."

Just as I said that, Diamond's phone went off and she lifted it, grinning again. I left her there in her happy little world. I needed to get some work done, so that I could head home and spend time with, Thee. I was missing him already.

-15-

Theory

"So, what's up? You and your girl good now?"
Frank and I were chilling at the bar having lunch at
Jimmy's, to kill time before I had to go see Alex's dumb
ass.

Frank lifted his beer, turned it up to finish it
before he held his hand up, signaling for the bartender.
"We're straight." The goofy ass grin on his face told a
different story. They were more than straight, but I left it
at that. If my man was good, then I was good.

"I'm just glad to see your ass happy. I didn't think
you would ever get your head right after Rachel." I lifted
my glass and spun it just a little, watching the ice bounce
off the sides before I turned it up.

"What can I get you, handsome?" Red asked, as
she leaned across the bar, exposing her nice, full breasts.
Red was cool as hell and flirted with me all the time, but
she knew her place. If she could have me, she would be
all in, but once I made it clear that all I needed from her
was to keep my drinks flowing, she kept it friendly. That
was hard to find in most females. Once they wanted you
and couldn't have you, they typically couldn't figure out
how to deal with you, without constantly crossing lines.
Red never did that. Aside from a little flirting, she kept it
moving.

"Let me get two more and you better put them damn things up before I latch on to one of them," Frank said, pointing at her chest.

Red laughed, lifted his empty beer bottles, and then smiled. "You can't handle me, Frank, but if you want me to bruise your ego then bring it." She winked at him and then walked off.

We both watched her thick thighs and ass, as she moved to the other end of the bar. Red was about a size twelve, thick, and sexy as fuck. She had a tiny waist leading up to her big ass breasts that were always on display. Red had a vanilla complexion and short hair that she kept flaming red, all the time. Her hazel eyes sat above a button nose, and thick, full lips.

"I can't believe you never fucked her, damn Thee. If I were you, I would have done that shit just out of curiosity. I know she's got some bomb ass pussy. I can tell just from watching her move."

I looked at Frank who was still watching Red, and laughed. "Nah, we cool and shit. I didn't want to fuck that up, but trust me, I thought about it. A lot." My eyes fell on Red who was leaning down to lift something off the floor.

"Nigga, I know your ass did. Shit, she fine as fuck, Thee." A few minutes later, she returned with his beers, grabbed my glass and set two beers in front of me. I smiled and nodded because she knew me.

"You know Rachel is part of the reason why I fixed shit with Diamond," Frank said, randomly.

I looked at him with my eyebrows raised. "Word, how the fuck that happen?"

He chuckled. "I was all fucked up after I left Diamond's apartment and for some reason, I thought about Rach. I called her and she knew something was bugging me. She wouldn't let it go, until I told her. She was all on that 'you need to find happiness' shit," he chuckled again, but this time because he was remembering their conversation.

"So, you let your ex talk you into fixing shit with your current girl. Damn Frank, your ass is playing with fire."

"Nah, it's not even like that. I'll always have love for Rachel, but she has babies with that nigga, two of them. I can't go there with her again, but I do miss that shit, though."

I looked at Frank, serious as hell. "You just make sure you miss that shit from a distance. The past is the past Frank, and I like Diamond. She's good for your simple ass."

"Fuck you, Thee, I got this shit. You just worry about convincing Rain to give your ugly ass that baby you want so bad."

"I don't have to convince her to do shit; it's happening." There was no questioning that. After almost losing my life, I started to realize that time isn't promised. I wanted to leave a legacy, but I couldn't do that without having a shorty.

I also wanted it all with Rain; marriage, kids, all the shit we both missed when we were kids. She was it for me, so there was no need to wait. I could already see her cute ass pregnant in my head, and a baby girl that looked just like her, or a son that acted just like me; well, almost like me. Hopefully, he would take on some of Rain's personality too, or I might have to fuck his little ass up.

"Yeah aight, I guess time will tell," Frank laughed.

We kicked it for a little while longer before I got ready to go see Alex. I was dreading that shit, but it had to be done. I had Niles and Frank's signatures, but I needed Alex to file the paperwork with the city so that it would be legal, and until I found a new lawyer, I had to deal with her dumb ass.

Just as I was about to enter the building where Alex's office was, Rain called. It was like she knew where I was and I almost started to look around to see if she was watching me.

"Hey, you." She was too damn happy to know that I was about to meet up with Alex.

"What's up, pretty?"

"I'm pretty?" she asked, with a light laugh.

"Actually, you're fucking beautiful and sexy as hell, but it would have taken too long to say all that."

"You're not so bad yourself." I could hear the smile in her voice. "Where are you?"

"About to go handle some stuff for the shop. What's up, you need me?" I asked, hoping the answer was no. I needed to get this handled with Alex.

"I always *need* you, but you told me I had to chill out until you were at one-hundred percent again," Rain said seductively, teasing me.

"See, there you go. Don't make me come down there and have your co-workers hear you hit them high notes. You trying to play."

Rain laughed. "You said that, not me."

"Yeah aight," I chuckled.

"Don't make plans for tomorrow. I have a work thing and I want you to go with me." I could tell from the way it came out that there was more to it. It was probably some fancy shit that I wasn't down for. I didn't have a problem getting fly, but that wasn't really my shit, but if my baby needed me to represent, then I was doing it.

"What kind of work thing?" I asked, trying to feel her out.

"Can we talk about it when we get home tonight?" She was lucky I wanted to get her off the phone so that I could go up here and see Alex. If Rain caught wind of where I was, she would have her hostile ass down here in a matter of seconds. Rain was chill for the most part, which I loved about her, but if you pissed her off, that was a different story. She was good with her hands, partly because of me, but then again she was a natural at that shit, too. Either way, Rain could fuck you up if given the opportunity, so I didn't want her anywhere near Alex, until I found a new lawyer.

"Yaeh, that's cool. I should be home early."

"Me, too. I don't have a lot going on today, but I need to go get some clothes."

"You need to stop fucking around and pack all your shit and just bring it home. And before you start with that slick ass mouth, yes, I said home. You live with me, so it's our home."

Rain laughed. "I wasn't going to say anything."

"Yes, the fuck you were, but it's all good. I love you, ma."

"I love you too, Thee."

I slid my phone in my pocket and hopped on the elevator. I hadn't talked to Alex since the whole thing went down in the hallway with her and that fuck nigga. I just hoped that she could get her feelings in check long enough to handle business. Shit, she already had my money, so like it or not, she was still my lawyer and going to do her fucking job.

"Hello, Mr. Bryant; she's in her office," Rissa said, with an awkward smile. I wasn't sure if she knew what was going on, but her desk was right near the front door, so it was likely she heard everything that went down with me, Alex, and Rain. If nothing else, she saw how I fucked that nigga up because he had to return to his office. I made my way to Alex's office and she was at her desk.

"Yes." Alex looked up at me with her face all scrunched up.

"Yo', kill the fucking attitude. I'm not paying you for that shit." I sat down in front of her and placed the folder that I had with the signed documents on her desk. She opened it and scanned through them, before looking right at me.

"So, I see you got Niles to sign these before you made him disappear," Alex said, with that funky ass attitude.

I glanced over my shoulder before I got up to close her door. Once it was shut, I walked around her desk and sat on the corner, letting my folded hands rest on my leg, while I peered at her.

"Look ma, I don't know what you think you know about Niles and I really don't give a fuck. What I pay you for is to keep my shit in order and legal, so that's the only thing that we're going to discuss. Is there any confusion about that?" I reached down and grabbed Alex by the cheap ass shirt she was wearing, lifting her a little as I pulled her towards me, so that I could look in her eyes.

"Yes, I'm sorry, I didn't mean…I'm sorry. No confusion," Alex began rambling when she realized how serious I was. I let her go and then returned to the opposite side of her desk and stood in front of it. She kept her eyes on me while she adjusted her clothes and tried to get herself together.

"Now, how long will it take you to get this handled?" I pointed to the file that I had just given her.

"Umm, about a week. I just have to file it and get the documents changed."

"Good, make that your priority. I'll check in with you soon, so don't call me. I don't have shit else to say to you right now, but when I do, I'll be in touch."

I moved to the door and once I had it open, I turned to look at Alex. "Oh, how's your nigga? I didn't fuck him up too bad, did I?" Alex's expression dropped and I could tell she wanted to say something, but knew better. I laughed and then left her office, feeling pleased. Now, it was off to my shop and then home later, to lay up under Rain.

*****

"Thee, come help me," I heard Rain yelling from downstairs, but she didn't seem like anything was wrong, so I took my time. I had been home for a few hours and crashed. I guess the rest I should have been getting, but wasn't, was starting to catch up with me because the second my head hit the pillow, I was out.

I sat up and stretched before I finally let my feet hit the floor. My body was healing, but still sore as hell, especially after I did a lot of moving around, and then was stationary for a while.

"Thee, are you sleep?" Rain yelled, this time a little louder.

"Chill ma, here I come." I slid my feet into my Nike slides and started towards my bedroom door. As soon as I was downstairs, I pulled Rain into my chest and kissed her. She hugged me back and looked up at me with a grin.

"I know you were sleep," she said, and then reached for my neck, letting her fingers glide across her name.

"You don't know shit," I said, and winked at her.

"I called you twice before I left Diamond's to see if you wanted me to get dinner, but you didn't answer, so you were sleep," she said over her shoulder, as she let me go and started towards the front door, so I followed.

"Maybe I was busy. Oh yeah, and don't go in the guest room until I can inspect it. You know how females be trying to leave shit to get you caught up."

I stopped on the porch and waited for her to respond.

"I wish you would; I would fuck you and the hoe up. Trust me, you don't want that."

"I mean, at least I respect you enough not to let it happen in our bed." I looked right at her, but she wasn't paying me any mind. She knew better and she knew for sure that I wouldn't cheat on her.

"Yeah, well I'll respect you enough not to fuck you in our bedroom anymore then." She looked right at me and then began pulling bags out of her back seat, and placing them on the ground.

I chuckled and joined her at the car, lifting the bags that she was sitting on the ground. "You can't live without this and you know it; talk is cheap, Rain." I turned to head towards the house carrying two suitcases and two duffle bags.

"Cheat on me and see," Rain yelled, as she ducked into her back seat to get more stuff.

Twenty minutes later, we had all of her things piled up on the floor of what was now our bedroom. I was happy as hell that she was moving in, while she was annoyed and complaining about what fact that she had just moved in with Diamond, and now was having to move all her stuff here.

"Why you complaining? You get to be here with me. That should make it all worthwhile," I said, as I stood over Rain. She was sitting on the floor surrounded by piles of clothes that she was trying to get organized enough to put away.

"Do you see this mess?" She leaned back, placing her arms behind her to balance her weight and then looked up at me like the world was about to end.

"I can pay somebody to do this shit for you, if you want?"

Now, she really had a sour look on her face. "That's just dumb and I don't want some random person going through my things."

"Then, stop damn complaining. Come on, you can do that later. Just chill with me for a little while, I missed you today."

"Thee, no, I need to get this done."

"Rain, that shit ain't going nowhere, come on."

She let out a frustrated breath before she finally gave in. After she was on her feet, I grabbed her hand and led her to the kitchen.

"I'm making dinner," I said, before I opened the refrigerator.

"You can't cook, Thee. I'm not in the mood for an emergency room visit."

"Shut the fuck up. I can't cook a lot, but I can rock with a few things."

"Like what?"

"You know, we used to eat that shit all the time," I said over my shoulder, while I scanned the contents of the refrigerator.

When I looked back at her, she had a confused stare on her face, but it turned into a grin.

"Grilled cheese and tomato soup," she said, with the biggest smile looking sexy as hell. I had to taste her lips, so I grabbed the butter and cheese, before I walked over to her and kissed her.

"Damn, that brings back a lot of memories." She smiled, likely thinking about how much we used to eat that shit. It was cheap and easy to make; loaf of bread and cheese would last us for a week.

"Hell, yeah. We didn't have shit, but we made it work." I chuckled, thinking about how messed up things used to be for us, but Rain never complained about any of it. As long as she had me she was good. That's how I knew she was everything to me. There weren't a lot of females that would have stuck with me like that. She could have easily left me on the streets and gone back into the system, but wherever I was, she was. That right there had a nigga willing to die to make sure she had any, and everything she ever wanted.

Rain walked over to me and hugged me from behind, pressing her body firmly against mine. I could feel her heart beating against my back and it did something to me. I could die today and know that I was loved in a way that only existed for a hand full of people.

Rain's Theory 2   K.C. Mills

That was unreal to me because it was almost like I didn't deserve it, but you better believe, I appreciated it.

16

Rain

"Don't they have anyone else that can do that shit?" I could hear the frustration in Theory's voice.

I looked across the room as he stripped out of his clothes. When he was down to just his boxer briefs, I bit my bottom lip and tried to focus on the disagreement we were having. I was struggling though, because he was so sexy, and then to add insult to injury, he was semi-hard, so I kept focusing on the imprint he was sporting.

"Rain, stop looking at my shit."

I tried to hide my grin while I looked up at him. "I know you don't want to go; I don't really want to go, but it's my job, Thee. What do you expect me to do?" I damn sure wasn't about to tell him that it wasn't even my assignment.

"It's not really about me. I don't give a fuck about Lani or her father. You know how I feel about all that extra shit. I don't fuck with that drama shit and you know, just like I know, that your ass is gonna be on one-hundred the second you lay eyes on her. I'm not in mood for that bullshit; it's not worth it."

"I don't care about her or her father either, but what I do care about is my job. I need to be there and I want you there with me, so can we not argue about this and just go."

Theory's hand went straight to his forehead, while he looked down at the floor and massaged his temple. After a few minutes of silence, he inhaled and let it out slow.

"This is not an argument, Rain. I'm just voicing my concerns. So, you really think you can be in a room with her and keep your damn hands to yourself?"

Nope, in fact I'm gonna slap the shit out of her as soon as I lay eyes on her. "I don't really have any fucks to give where she's concerned, but I am smart enough to know that I have to be professional, so yeah, I can handle myself."

Theory was still across the room and I couldn't take my eyes off him. This man was cut to perfection, not bulky with excessive muscle, but he was far from skinny. His build was right there in the middle, just like I liked it. His chest and arms nicely defined, while the muscles in his thighs and calves, were just right. Good Lord, I was in love with every inch of his body.

"I'm telling you now, if you get in there showing your ass I'm gonna be pissed, and I'm dragging you up out of there. That bitch can act as crazy as she wants because I don't give a fuck about her, but you represent me, ma. I don't do all that extra shit and trust me, they might not have had a reason to fire your ass before, but if you get in there putting your hands on his daughter, I promise, he'll find a way. I can't fix everything, so think about that before you get the urge to show your ass."

I just laughed because he was serious, but it was cute. The way he was trying to handle me, in only a way that Theory could. True indeed, he wasn't the type to deal with bullshit, but he was more concerned about me. He knew me and he knew that I was going in on Lani, if I got the chance. If that happened then he was right, I could lose my job, and legitimately this time. He didn't always do things the way most people did, but everything Theory did was out of love for me.

Theory looked at me for a few more seconds before he made his way to the bathroom. Just before he entered, he stopped and turned to face me.

"Oh, and you can stop eye fucking me because you can't have this shit until later, since we have to go to this bullshit, so before you start pouting about it, blame your damn self."

He looked so frustrated that I burst out laughing, which he didn't appreciate. The bathroom door slammed and I laid back and relaxed.

*****

"Aye sexy, you look good, boo." Diamond grabbed both of my hands and held them out beside me. I was dressed in a pair of black skinny jeans with a silver sheer top that attached around my neck and waist, so that my entire back was exposed.

"You too, Dia, you're killing that dress." Diamond was in a red bandage dress that stopped mid-thigh, and a pair of heels that I would have broken my neck in. Frank and Theory were at the bar, while we were standing a few feet away. Theory had my camera over his shoulder, looking sexy as ever, in a pair of dark jeans, a wheat-colored linen polo button-up, with a matching pair of wheat Timbs, on his feet. He was dressed simple, but he was wearing that shit. I couldn't help but crave him every time I looked his way.

"It's so crowded in here. I guess they're feeling Jax, huh?" I said, scanning the club. The atmosphere was chill and laid back, but the drinks were plentiful and the dance floor was full. Jax's album was playing and it sounded even better as it filled the club. I smiled at the promo shots that I took of Jax in the studio that were hanging in various spots. This is what it was all about; the reason why I worked so hard and loved my job.

"I know right. His sexy ass," Diamond said, and then winked at me.

"The fuck you over here grinning about?" Frank asked, as he walked up behind Diamond and kissed her on the neck. He handed her a glass, which she accepted and immediately took a sip of. Theory followed suit and handed me a drink and then let his arm fall around my waist, before he pressed his body against mine. I inhaled his cologne and smiled.

"I was thinking about you, sexy," Diamond held her head back so that she could look up at Frank.

He blushed a little. "What the fuck, ever. I know your ass is in here checking out other niggas."

Diamond turned to face Frank and pecked him on the lips. "Why would I do that? Nobody in here has a damn thing on you."

"Go on with that bullshit," Frank said, but he leaned down and kissed her a little deeper.

"Aye, y'all so cute."

Diamond turned to me and laughed before rolling her eyes. "It's not the same when you say it."

I took a sip of the drink Theory handed me. "What's this?" I asked, looking down at my glass. I wasn't much of a drinker, but this was sweet and I liked it.

"A mimosa, it's not that strong. You're supposed to be working so I don't need you in here getting fucked up." Theory leaned down and kissed my temple.

"Hell, you know she's a light weight, that's probably still too much," Diamond said, causing Theory to chuckle.

"Well, everyone can't be like you, Diamond," I said, just as she turned up her glass to finish off the rest of her drink.

"How about you kiss my ass," Diamond shot me a bird.

"I guess I better go find Jax so I can get started." I pulled away from Theory, but he caught my waist and pulled me back towards him.

"No, *we* are going to find Jax. I can't trust you alone up in here."

Diamond laughed. "Well, we're going to dance."

"No the hell we're not," Frank said, looking down at Diamond like she was crazy.

"You really want me on the dance floor alone, looking like this?" Diamond shifted all of her weight to one leg, popping her hip, while holding her hands out.

"Aye, you better handle that bruh," Theory looked at Frank and laughed.

I could tell that Frank was not feeling the idea of being on a dance floor, but he went because he damn sure didn't want her out there alone.

"Let's go." Theory took my hand and started leading the way towards the area that was set up for Jax.

"You know you don't have to babysit me. I told you I wasn't worried about your little friend."

"What I tell you about that. She ain't *my* anything and this don't have shit to do with her. I don't know who this nigga is and you up in here half-dressed. Wherever you are, I am."

I laughed. My baby was jealous, but it was cute on him, though. We made our way to Jax's area and he was there surrounded by a bunch of people, but the second he saw me, he came over to speak.

"Hey, you made it," Jax said, the second he was in front of us, but his first move was to extended a hand to Theory to introduce himself. That was a respect thing and I was glad that Jax understood protocol.

"I'm Jax." Theory accepted his hand, but his body language was still defensive and protective. He was holding me so close to his side, that we were damn near one.

"What's good, bruh. You got a big crowd here tonight." I laughed to myself noticing that Theory didn't offer his name. He was still feeling Jax out and didn't deem him worthy yet. I had seen him do that plenty of times before.

"Yeah, it's straight. I appreciate you letting her come out tonight. I hated to switch shit up like that, but dude wasn't on his shit, so I asked Rain."

Oh shit. Theory looked at me, but then went right back to Jax, "Oh, yeah?"

"Yeah, so when I called and she accepted, I was truly appreciative." Jax was totally throwing me under the bus and had no idea. *Fuck.*

He finally looked down and focused on me. "Just do your thing and shoot whatever you feel is relevant. I guess I need to be in a few shots, but other than that, just do what you do. Oh, and I think your sister is around here somewhere."

"Okay, thanks."

"Alright, let me get back to it. Have fun, if you need anything let me know." Just like that Jax was gone, and Theory was looking at me like he wanted to wrap his hands around my neck.

"So, he called you personally and asked you to do this shit?" Theory looked pissed.

"Yeah, but it's not even what you're thinking, so calm down," I said, before this situation got out of hand.

"The fuck you mean calm down. I'm not upset. I'm just trying to figure out why your ass was breaking your neck to come do this shit, when you really didn't have to."

"I didn't have to, but he asked and I—"

"You know what, fuck it. I guess you doing your own thing. That's cool." Theory turned to walk off, but I grabbed his hand to stop him. I probably should have told him, but I knew for sure if I did that he wasn't going to want me to do it. I needed the exposure and this was a huge event.

"Thee, wait, please."

"For what? You obviously got shit figured out so my vote don't count." His deep voice cut though the noise in the club.

"Don't do that. That's not us."

"No, Rain, this shit is not us; you lying to me is not us!" he yelled.

"I didn't lie, Thee, I just didn't tell you all the details. I accepted the assignment so I had to be here."

Theory laughed, sarcastically. "Don't matter how you spin that shit Rain. You weren't being honest and what the fuck does he mean by your sister? You got a lot of damn secrets."

"I don't have secrets. Don't try to make it something it's not."

"Do you have a sister that I don't know about?"

Theory waited for me to answer.

"Technically, yes."

"Then, technically your ass got secrets. It's cool though. Go do your damn thing, ma. You got work to do, right? Isn't that why you had to be here?" I could hear the sarcasm in his voice which hurt a little, but it was my fault; I couldn't really say a damn thing. Theory looked at me in a way that had my heart aching. I could still see the love he had for me, but it was hidden behind the anger he was feeling right now.

Theory lifted my camera from his shoulder and handed it to me before he kissed me on the forehead. "Go do your thing Rain. I'll be at the bar."

He turned to walk away and I knew better than to go after him because when Theory was like this, he wasn't going to talk, until he was ready. At this point, all I could do was my job, so I turned on my camera and went to work.

17

Theory

I was fucking fuming. I already didn't want to be here and then come to find out, Rain did this shit as a personal favor for this damn nigga. I didn't know what the fuck was up with that shit, but it had me wanting to load his ass up with lead. I never thought that I had to worry about Rain doing any fuck shit like that, but this situation was just disrespectful as hell. There was no reason at all for us to be here, yet she felt the need to be doing personal favors for another muthafucker.

I didn't even care about the fact that she had a sister and didn't tell me, but it just hit at the right time, so I added that shit in there too. I knew it had to be an adopted sister because I knew for a fact that Rain was an only child.

"Yo', the fuck you sitting here looking like you want to fuck shit up?"

Frank sat down next to me at the bar while I looked across it. It didn't matter how pissed I was with Rain; I still wasn't going to let shit happen to her or let another muthafucker push up on her. The second I laid eyes on her and saw that she was good, chilling with Diamond, I focused on Frank.

"Just some bullshit, not even worth mentioning." I lifted my glass and turned it up before I set it down in front of me again.

"If it has you over here looking like you 'bout to blow this bitch up, then it's worth mentioning. Talk nigga." Frank held his hand in the air to signal for the bartender and then looked at me. I saw Diamond place her hands on her hips and then look our way like she was pissed.

"What can I get you?" a guy asked, when he made it over to Frank.

"Hennessy and bring the bottle." Frank glanced at him, and then the bartender nodded and walked off. He returned a few minutes later with a glass and a bottle of Hennessy, which he placed in front of Frank. Frank reached in his pocket, retrieved a stack of bills and then handed the guy a few. He nodded and walked off.

"I'm waiting." Frank filled his glass and then turned to look at me.

"The only reason why we're here is because that nigga called her personally to ask her to do this shit," I pointed to one of the stand-ups of Jax.

"Wait, I thought this was a work thing?"

"It is, but only because he requested her and asked her personally. She conveniently left that shit out. She made it seem like she didn't have a choice."

Frank laughed and I wanted to rock the shit out of his ass because there wasn't a damn thing funny.

"Yo', you need to calm the fuck down. Rain don't want that nigga. Look at him Thee, his pretty ass looks like a damn girl." I looked at Frank hard as hell, but couldn't hold it because he was right. That nigga was pretty as shit.

"You're dumb as fuck. It's not about whether or not she wants him, she just don't need to be doing favors for no man, I don't give a fuck who he is. That's just disrespectful because you know niggas be taking that as a sign that females wanna fuck."

"True, but you know that ain't your girl, Thee. Rain don't get down like that. She don't see nobody, but your ugly ass, no matter who's around."

I laughed. "Call me ugly one more damn time and I'm going to fuck you up."

"What the fuck ever, but chill with that. You know she don't want nobody, but you. Yeah, it was disrespectful, but that's all it was. I don't see motive there."

"Yeah, but trust me if it's business, then they need to be calling on a business phone, not her personal damn cell phone. That shit is dead."

"I feel you on that," Frank said and laughed.

"Hey, sexy. You don't need to be over here all alone like this. How about we go hit the dance floor."

"Nah, ma, I'm good."

I knew whoever was all in my personal space was talking to me, but I wasn't interested so I didn't bother looking her way.

"You can at least look in my eyes and decide before you say no." I felt a hand on my chest, which I caught and shoved away. I turned to face her, but my answer didn't change.

"I said, I'm good, ma."

I looked right into a pretty mocha-colored face that was staring back at me, seductively. She had short cropped hair that was laid, with thin slanted eyes. I could tell she was mixed with something because of her round, flat face, slanted eyes and thin lips. She was cute, but too aggressive and most importantly, not Rain.

"So, you can just look at me and tell me no." My eyes roamed her body and I had to admit it was nice. If she had caught me before Rain showed up I might have fucked her, but I could also tell that she had an agenda. I looked like money and she was on the prowl for dollar signs.

"Yeah, ma, I can look at you and tell you no. You're pretty, so I know you're used to niggas falling for that shit, but all I see when I look at you is a pussy with a lot of miles on it."

Her mouth fell open and she stood there for a minute, not knowing what to say. Luckily, her friend walked up and saved her.

"Charlotte, Jax is looking for you. Who's this?" she asked, when she noticed me.

"I'm nobody, ma." I turned to focus on Frank again who was laughing.

"Damn, you're rude," her friend said.

I just chuckled. I was rude because I didn't want their hoe asses. That shit was funny.

"Damn, Thee, you didn't have to do that damn girl like that. You could have told her you weren't interested.

"Shit, I did that, but she obviously wasn't trying to hear that, so I had to make sure I was real clear."

"Nah, your ass did exactly what you were trying to do and that was hurt her damn feelings."

"I want her out." I heard a female voice yell and just like I thought, I looked up and saw Lani, pointing at Rain, with her father standing right behind her.

"Fuck! See, this is exactly why I didn't want to be here. I knew this shit was going to happen."

Frank finished his drink and we both hauled ass towards Rain and Lani. I had my eyes on her the entire time and they were going back and forth, until Lani reached out like she was about to hit Rain, but that nigga Jax came out of nowhere and grabbed Lani's hand. This situation went from bad to worse.

The second I was near Rain, I stepped in between her and Jax, making sure I made contact with him, shoving his ass out the way.

"What I tell you about that shit. I told you if you ever put your hands on her then you would have to deal with me." I pointed my finger at Lani and she backed up, stepping slightly behind her dad.

I chuckled. "The fuck you stepping behind him for. I'll fuck him up, too."

Frank was by my side with his hand on his waist, just in case.

"Bitch, I wish you would touch my girl. You'll be all kinds of fucked up," Diamond yelled.

"She ain't crazy, trust that." Now here goes Rain.

I looked down at Rain to let her know to calm that shit down while Frank did the same for Diamond. We were not about to be typical niggas up in a club fighting.

"I think you need to leave. All of you," Detroit said, looking right at me.

"First of all, you can't tell me shit. If I want to leave, I will, but not because of your pedophile ass."

Detroit looked around trying to see who was listening. We were in one of the corners of the club with very few people, so no one was really paying attention to us.

"This is my photographer. She's working and your daughter tried to put her hands on her."

This nigga did not understand how to stay in his fucking lane. I didn't need him defending Rain.

"Yo, she's good, bruh. I got this," I said, looking him right in the eye, so that he would understand I meant business.

He held his hands up and stepped back. At least he had that much respect.

"You got what you need?" I looked across my shoulder at Rain who was standing slightly behind me. I knew her ass was ready to jump on Lani, but I wasn't having that shit. I had no doubt that Rain would fuck her up, but I just couldn't get with that hood shit, not up in here. There was forever somebody with a damn cell phone and I wasn't about to have Rain's ass up on *World Star*.

"Yeah, I'm good," she said.

"Frank?" I looked at him and nodded towards Rain. He stepped closer to her while I took a step towards Detroit.

"Fuck with her job again if you want to and I promise you will regret the day you met me."

I made sure we were inches apart because I had him in height by about a foot and a half. I could see the fear in his eyes, which made me laugh before I stepped back and grabbed Rain's hand.

"Let's go."

She looked up at me like she wanted to say something, but she followed, until Lani's stupid ass called her a bitch, and Rain yanked away from me and hit Lani with a two-piece that had to have broken her damn nose.

"I'll be a bitch, but this bitch is good with her hands," Rain said with a smirk, before I snatched her little ass up so that we could leave.

Once we were outside the club and Frank finally got Diamond calmed down enough for all of us to head home, we said our goodbyes and Rain and I left in my truck. The ride was quiet, only because I wasn't really saying anything and Rain thought I was mad at her. I low key was about the Jax thing, but I was happy as hell she punched Lani in her damn face because I couldn't, and I wanted to.

After we were inside, Rain went right to our room, while I stayed in the kitchen. I needed a drink and I wanted her to sweat it out a little longer. She just kept looking at me on the drive home, but wouldn't say anything. I could tell she was hoping I would break first, which I usually did. Rain would rather take an argument and get it over with, than for me not to talk to her. I knew this was fucking with her, but that was exactly what I wanted.

After about an hour later, I was sitting at the kitchen table going through my messages, when I heard Rain's voice.

"Are you not coming to bed?" She walked over to me, but stopped about a foot away. She was dressed for bed and I could smell her body wash.

I just looked up at her and then focused on my phone again, without saying anything. I wasn't mad, I was just fucking with her.

"Thee, don't do that." She stepped closer and climbed in my lap, straddling my thighs, looking up at me with pouting lips, before placing her hands on my shoulders.

I leaned back, kept my expression hard and just stared at her.

"So, you're really not going to talk to me?" She frowned, sticking her lips out a little further. All I could think about at that point was sucking on them.

"Are you really doing personal favors for other niggas?" I asked, grabbing her hands to remove them from my shoulders."

"It's not like that, and I hope you know I don't want or need anything from him. In fact, he's my sister's boyfriend."

I laughed, sarcastically. "Do you know how many muthafuckers dream about fucking sisters. You think that means something? Look, it was disrespectful as hell and the fact that you had to hide it tells me that you knew that, but I'm over that shit. I can tell you this though, if it's business, then they need to be calling your fucking job and not your damn cell phone. When niggas get personal like that, they read into that shit. You might not have intentions, but it doesn't mean that they don't, so keep it professional."

I pulled Rain into my body and kissed her on the lips. She released a smile and then laid her head on my shoulder.

"I'm sorry if I made you doubt me."

"We're good, just let it go. What's the deal with your sister?"

Rain looked up at me and her expression dropped before she shrugged. "There's really nothing up with us. We're not that close."

"But, she's here? Have you talked to her?"

"I didn't know she was here until my mom told me just recently, and then I saw her at the shoot we did for Jax. I haven't talked to her though, and honestly, I probably won't."

"Why aren't you close?" I knew Rain didn't really fuck with too many people, but she was generally a chill person, so she was cool with everybody. It didn't mean she would hang tight with you, but she didn't really have issues with most people.

"She's just never really liked me. She was there first, so when they adopted me, she felt like I took all of her attention. They loved us both, but in different ways. I never really did anything, while Charlotte was into everything, so that meant they were constantly on her. She, of course, took that to mean that they loved me, and hated her."

"I can see how that could affect things, but you're older now, so maybe things are different."

"I doubt it, but either way, I don't really care. I'm good, with or without her."

I looked at Rain and laughed. "Come on, let's go to bed. I'm tired as fuck and ready for this day to be done.

We made our way upstairs and Rain climbed in bed, while I showered. Once I was dressed, I joined her and pulled her body into mine. My hands glided across her soft skin, while I focused on the sound of her breathing. If I could have this forever, then nothing else would matter. I closed my eyes and was out before I could process anything else.

*****

I could hear Rain's phone going off and knew that it was late, so I immediately thought something was wrong. When I finally heard her voice, we both sat up at the same time.

"Who is this? What's wrong? Where's Jax? What about your friends Charlotte, don't you have anyone else to call? Fine, where are you? It's going to take me a minute, but I'll be there. Yeah, okay." I listened to the part of the conversation that I could hear, trying to piece it together, and it sounded like it was her sister.

"Oh my God, you have got to be fucking kidding me." Rain dropped her phone on the bed and sighed.

"Who was that?" I asked.

"My sister."

Rain threw the covers back and aggressively climbed out of bed.

"The fuck you going?" I asked following her lead.

"To get her. She's stuck at some hotel, alone. She got into it with Jax and he left her at the club, so she left with some guy she didn't know and ended up at a hotel, with nothing. I don't even know the rest or care, but she wants me to come get her because she doesn't have anyone else to call, or anywhere to go. Imagine that." She mumbled at the end, more to herself than to me.

"Aight then, let me get dressed because you're damn sure not going alone.

"This right here is exactly why we don't get along," Rain said, just before she walked into the bathroom.

After we were dressed, Rain's sister texted her the name and location of the hotel, so we left to go get her. It was three in the morning and Rain was pissed, but because of who she was and no matter what she felt about her sister, Rain wasn't going to leave her hanging. That was just who Rain was, and I loved her for that. She was selfless and it was a quality that you couldn't take for granted, because it was so rare.

It took us about forty-five minutes to get to where her sister was and after we parked, Rain and I got out to walk to the room that she was in. Apparently, the dude left and told her that he would be back with some friends, and she didn't have a car to leave, so she was stuck. Rain's sister had apparently moved here to be with Jax and was living off his dime, so without him she didn't have shit.

"Thank you." Rain looked back at me and smiled just before she knocked on the door that her sister was in.

I leaned down and kissed her on the cheek. "For what? I got you with whatever you need and you don't have to thank me for that." I winked at Rain and she knocked on the door. It opened a few minutes later and I was face to face with shorty from the club. She looked up at me and smiled like she hit the fucking lottery, while I looked down at her, like I just got robbed. *Let the bullshit begin.*

Join our mailing list to get a notification when Leo Sullivan Presents has another release!

Text LEOSULLIVAN to 22828 to join!

To submit a manuscript for our review, email us at leosullivanpresents@gmail.com

Coming Soon from Sullivan Productions!

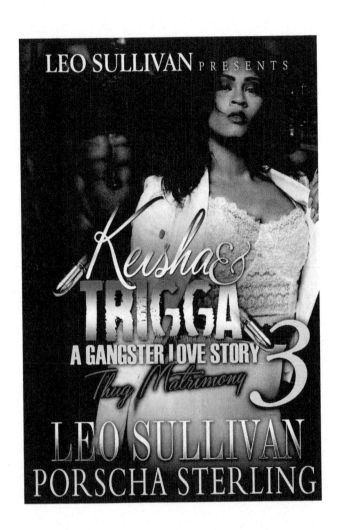

CPSIA information can be obtained
at www.ICGtesting.com
Printed in the USA
LVOW04s1737021216
515533LV00009B/556/P